ZULU WAR

Jabulani,
Africa 1879-1882

by Vince Cross

D0928778

SCHOLASTIC

To Amy, Michael, Catherine, Ruth, Peter and Veronica
With thanks for opening my eyes

While the events described and some of the characters in this book may be based
on actual historical events and real people, Jabulani is a fictional character, created
by the author, and his story is a work of fiction.

Scholastic Children's Books
Commonwealth House, 1–19 New Oxford Street,
London, WC1A 1NU, UK
A division of Scholastic Ltd
London ~ New York ~ Toronto ~ Sydney ~ Auckland
Mexico City ~ New Delhi ~ Hong Kong

Published in the UK by Scholastic Ltd, 2002

Copyright © Vince Cross, 2002

ISBN 0 439 98107 7

Printed and bound in Great Britain by Mackays of Chatham Limited, Chatham, Kent

Cover image: Young Zulu Warrior, Mary Evans Picture Library.
Background image: Peter Newark's Pictures.
2 4 6 8 10 9 7 5 3 1

The right of Vince Cross to be identified as the author of this work has been
asserted by him in accordance with the Copyright, Designs and Patents Act, 1988.

May 1882

My name is Jabulani, son of Sihayo. My father's voice is louder than the thunder which echoes around the eagles' crest. His strength is more than a lion thrusting at the kill. He is as cunning and wise as a black mamba hiding in the branches of a forest tree, waiting for its prey. All I want is that one day I shall be as great as he. All I dream is that one day I can add shining glory to my famous ancestors' memory by my deeds. And maybe one day when I am gone I shall be praised by my sons and grandsons in their turn.

When I was four years old and still clinging to my mother's knees, a *sangoma* who visited our hut searched deeply into my eyes and said it would be so. My older brothers can tease me about it now, but the words were spoken, and they can't be unsaid. If I keep myself pure, if I listen to my ancestors, if I work hard and show courage, the prophecy is that one day I'll be honoured as my great father Sihayo's equal.

I'm nearly sixteen now. If I weren't trapped here, pacing the deck of a British boat bound for a faraway

English port, I would show you how I can run like the wind. I'm tall and strong. I'm better than any boy of my age at throwing a spear. When it comes to fighting with a staff, no one from my year group, my *intanga*, can challenge me. For the time being I may be a mere *udibi* bringing food and sleeping mats to King Cetshwayo in his ship-prison. But one day I have it within me to be the finest Zulu warrior. In my heart I know it. In my heart I have already washed my spear in blood.

Let me tell you the story of how the King and I came to be here, far from our beloved country, pitching and rolling on this great grey-green ocean.

Early January 1879

Something was wrong. An odd, brooding atmosphere drifted around me like a cloud from the grazing lands that sloped away down the far side of Skull Hill. I took a little more care than usual as I swung my legs across the awkward, jagged rocks which keep the entrance to my cave safe.

It's not really my cave. I expect everyone in the village knows about it. Skull Hill looms up to the south-west above the gorge where our *kraal* sits. It's a short steep walk to the top. The cave lies just below the summit, facing the gorge on a ledge, but hidden by a screen of rubble. The first time I went inside, when I was very small, I felt it was very special to me. I used to go there every day if I could, for a little time alone with my ancestors, to learn at their feet, to become strong.

Perhaps that day without realizing it, I'd actually smelt the strangers beyond me on the hill, out of sight of the *kraal*. Or perhaps it was the total quietness that made me beware. I remember wondering where the birds had gone. It was just after dawn and the coarse black-green grass was soaked with the overnight rain. They should have been singing their hearts out!

Then as I clambered up over the summit, I saw the grassland on the far side was empty, and my chest pounded. There were no cattle to be seen anywhere. I turned around, shielding my eyes from the low sun, but saw no reassuring brown shapes, heard no welcome lowing. I'd left them safely the previous evening, and now they were gone.

It had to be one of two things. Either one of my brothers was playing a trick, or our cows had been stolen. But who would do that? My father Sihayo had no enemies as far as I knew.

For a moment I stood and looked around hopelessly, scouring the rocks and the horizon for a sign of movement. Nothing stirred. I rubbed my eyes, as if it was possible this was a bad dream and I'd wake myself up. I thumped my fist into my side. Why did I have to be in charge, when ten precious head of cattle decided to go missing? Cattle are wealth to us. We have nothing but cattle. We need nothing else. They give us food and drink. They pull our ploughs. When they die their hide makes clothing and shields for warriors.

If my brothers had set me a test, I knew I had to be

equal to it. If the cattle had been stolen, I wanted to know by whom. Either way, I had to find the missing beasts and quickly.

Years ago the cattle were kept in the *kraal* every night, so my brothers had told me, because it was the only way they could be safe then. For a while there'd been trouble with other tribes, when the rains had failed and people had been starving. But in my lifetime there'd been no raids over the border from Natal and the cattle had been free to roam the grasslands around our *kraal*. It's far better for animals to have a little freedom on the hills and enjoy the bright shoots of the young grass before the days of unrelenting sun scorch them off. You can almost hear the grass growing while the rains fall. The plants drink in the precious moisture and shout for joy.

I ran stealthily along towards a crag where I knew I could safely scan a long stretch of valley without being seen. To my right the stream which supplies our *kraal* tumbled out of the gorge into the great *Mzinyathi*, the Buffalo River which makes the border between the land of the Zulus and Natal. To my left the river curved away to the south-east. What I saw in that direction took my breath away. Deep in the shadow of the line of hills and on the Zulu side of the river, straggled a column of white man's wagons and horses more than 100 paces long. In between the wagons was a herd of cattle. The more I looked, the more I was sure those were my cows down there, now just ten faces amongst a larger crowd, probably being jostled and kicked by strangers who couldn't understand their ways, and wouldn't know their names. There was movement in the column. The men seemed to be saddling up to drive the cattle back over the border into Natal.

Even from where I stood I could tell these men weren't like the white man I knew best. Father Simons lived at the mission station by the end of the gorge – still lives there as far as I know – and he's a good, kind and gentle man. I've learnt so much from him, so many wonderful facts, so many strange ideas. And my English of course, of which I'm so proud! From the very first time he met me when I was just six years old and he was struggling to build his house, there was a closeness between us. I brought him water as he toiled under the hot sun. And it was through me that he became friends with my father.

The top halves of the bodies of these white men were covered in patched red jackets, their legs wrapped in mud-spattered trousers that might once have been blue. Each man shouldered a rifle. I'd seen pictures of men like these in the books on Father Simon's wooden shelves. They probably weren't good, kind and gentle. They were the white man's warriors, and if they were here they must have come to do us harm.

For a brief moment I couldn't help standing and watching. Then I remembered my duty and leaped back up over the rocks, hurtling down the hill to warn my family and confess my shame at the loss of the cattle.

I ran very fast. I've always had well-muscled calves and tough skin, and when I was little my elders used to growl at me, "More haste, less speed, Jabulani!" as I fell over cooking pots and broke fences. I was always so keen to be somewhere else – and quickly. But I've rarely run as I did that day. The rocks and thorns meant nothing to my flying feet.

That's another thing about white men and their clothing. Why do they all wear those hot, heavy boots? Are they afraid of snakes? If you're careful, you'll never step on a snake in the bush. But you can't run or balance if your feet are imprisoned in leather. Trust me! I've tried it and I know.

I bolted down the side of the gorge on to the

platform of land where the 30 or so huts of kwaSihayo lie. On the way to it, I flew past my friend Sipho.

"What's the hurry?" he asked. "And why are you down here anyway? You'll be in trouble if your brother Nkubikazulu sees you."

I was gasping for breath now. "That's who I'm looking for!" I panted. "Where is he?"

"They're all up at *nkosi*'s tree," said Sipho, pointing. It was obvious he was dying to know quite what was so important, but there was no time to gossip.

My father has a favourite tree, where he goes to think and consult, and so the place has become known as "*nkosi*'s tree". My father Sihayo is truly "*nkosi*" to us all. He's a wealthy man, a man of influence, a friend and advisor to King Cetshwayo, a wise father to his family. However he and my eldest brother Mehlokazulu had left to see the King days ago. So I was curious. Why had Nkubikazulu, the next eldest brother and so the next most senior man in the village, taken himself off to my father's special tree? And who was there with him?

I sped on through the huts, vaulted the fence, and ran out to where a knot of men were squatting underneath the shade-giving branches. I sat myself down, and at the first pause in conversation, apologized breathlessly for disturbing them. Although I was frightened that Nkubikazulu would be angry and punish me for being careless with the cattle, I launched into my tale.

Loud "*Ay-ih*'s" and much sucking of teeth accompanied my telling of what I'd seen. Then every eye turned towards Nkubikazulu. He took the piece of grass he'd been chewing out of his mouth and spat. His eyes narrowed and my heart thumped a war dance. Nkubikazulu was the hot-head of the family, famous for his terrible temper, but his first words were to the group of elders, not me, and they were quietly spoken.

"So it's true then," he said grimly, looking around and nodding his head. "Just as my father Sihayo predicted, the white men have come. You see what I mean. We must prepare for the worst."

The others sighed in sad agreement.

Then he spoke to me. He could see I was trembling. "Don't be afraid, little brother! You did what you could. You came quickly to tell us what you saw, and you hid nothing. That was well done."

I shook my head. "I should have been there to stop them," I said fiercely, and banged my fist into the ground. I really meant it.

The fire in my voice drew a chuckle from the elders, and a belly laugh from Nkubikazulu.

"I think," he said slowly, "it's a good thing you weren't, young Jabulani!" When the elders eventually rose to go back to their huts, he spoke to me by myself. "It's no great surprise," he whispered. "Something like this has been expected ever since our mother Kaqwelebana's disgrace." He pointed a bony arm up to the north. "Why do you think all the rest of the cattle are grazing on the other side of the gorge? Your father told us this would happen. He said a bit of cattle-rustling might be a first warning of greater troubles to come. Haven't you noticed we've spread them out a little more during these last weeks?" He shrugged his shoulders. "Don't take it to heart. In the end it's only a few cows. Better we lose cattle than men."

I was puzzled.

"Are you saying the red soldiers are here because of Kaqwelebana?" I asked in amazement. "After all this time?"

"What she did was always going to bring the sky down on the Zulu people," said Nkubikazulu, with a bitter edge to his voice. "Our mother had no shame. And she has brought shame on us."

I felt my cheeks flush. For all her faults, it still made

me uncomfortable to hear my mother spoken of like that.

"So is *she* the reason why my father and Mehlokazulu are with the King?" I said. "Tell me, Nkubikazulu! What's going on?"

He leaned towards me. "It's no longer just in the family, Jabulani. What was sown last winter may reap a bitter harvest for all Zulus. Do you understand?"

I didn't understand, not really. Yes, six months previously I'd been there with Mehlokazulu, Nkubikazulu and the rest. I knew how they'd taken revenge on Kaqwelebana. But it had nothing to do with anyone outside kwaSihayo, and particularly not the white men. This was our pain and no one else's. Or so I thought.

Let me tell you how that pain came to settle on our *kraal*.

As befits a great chief, my father Sihayo had several wives, but my mother, Kaqwelebana, had been his Great Wife. She'd personally borne him four sons and I was the last, the surprise, a gift to his old age. The other wives were younger and more obviously beautiful, but Kaqwelebana was the jewel of the family, so my father had often said in the old days. Obviously he knew a different person than the one I saw.

With me she was always cold and distant, haughty and unkind. I never knew why and when I was small it made me cry. If I'm honest, Thabi, the next most senior wife, was more a mother than Kaqwelebana ever was.

You didn't argue with Kaqwelebana. She ran the home affairs of the entire village by her big stick. Woe betide any junior wife or child who slacked in sweeping the huts or hoeing the fields. Kaqwelebana's beatings were legendary and to be avoided at all costs. The bruises lasted a month.

As I grew up and left the care of the women, I could see that Kaqwelebana was becoming increasingly lazy, fat and unreasonable. More and more, she just sat at the door of her large hut next to Sihayo's, where she could see everything that went on, and held court.

For all that she was so horrible, her methods worked. The large circle of huts that made up our *umuzi* was always clean and tidy. We were never short of food, even in years when the rains were reluctant to come. People from the various families were nice to

14

each other. Of course they were! They feared for their lives if they weren't. And that included the men! Even they found themselves cowering away from a shower of insults if Kaqwelebana decided they were good-for-nothings.

I was still in my eleventh year when I first heard the tittle-tattle about my mother.

Sipho dug me in the ribs one day. "What's Kaqwelebana up to then?" he said as we practised with our spears one afternoon. He rolled a very over-ripe melon down the hillside 30 paces, and invited me to throw. The shaft of my spear bounced on the melon's rump, and then skittered on down the stony path. I hissed disappointment at my poor aim.

"How should I know?" I said.

"I thought everyone did," he teased.

"Well, not me," I said crossly, not liking being the last to know about anything. I should have known. Sipho had a talent for gossip.

"The girls think she's fallen in love," Sipho continued with a mischievous smile. I stared at him, as unbelieving as if he'd told me the river had started to run with milk rather than water.

"You're mad," I said. "She's old!"

"Old ... and in love!" insisted Sipho. "Girls always

know about these things." He released his spear. It cut an arc through the air and sank into the melon with a satisfying splat. A mess of seeds and juice burst on to the path.

"Well, who with?" I said, still not believing him. "Who'd be stupid enough?"

Sipho told me that the person in question was a distant relation of my father's, a younger man, handsome and strong but not very clever. But then, we laughed, Kaqwelebana probably wasn't interested in his brains. His name was Mbopa. Dopey Mbopa, we'd always called him.

Over the weeks the whispering continued, and worse than before, the rumours began to include Mbopa's brother Mgobe. It was suggested he was visiting Sibongile, another of Sihayo's wives, and all this behind my father's back. He was often away attending King Cetshwayo at the royal palace in Ulundi.

Kaqwelebana's grip on the village began to loosen. The women would smile a knowing smile at her and be just that little bit slower to do as they were told. People stopped talking when Sipho and I passed close by, and then started muttering to each other again when they thought we were out of earshot.

Mehlokazulu, my eldest brother, seemed to carry a face like thunder around with him all the time.

One night, while Sihayo was still away, there was a sudden commotion on the far side of the village from the hut where I slept with Sipho and other boys of our age group. Men shouted and women screamed. It sounded as if murder was being done, or a wild pig skinned alive, and we poked our heads round the corner to see if we were under attack.

"It's Kaqwelebana," said Sipho gleefully, as we peered into the night, "getting what she deserves at last! I'd know her voice anywhere."

"Don't we all!" said another of the boys sleepily.

"It's my mother you're talking about," I said.

"Fine mother she is!" Sipho teased.

"Shut up, or I'll sort you all out!" I replied sharply. There are some things you can think yourself, and other people shouldn't say.

I could hear Mehlokazulu's voice raised above everyone else's, then some footsteps running, crashing into the bush, followed by others. After that, until dawn the only sounds that broke the silence of the night were occasional low murmurings among the men.

The camp was buzzing with the scandal next morning. I felt uneasy about it all. My mother was still my mother, whatever she'd done. I cornered Thabi and tried to get her to talk. At first she wouldn't.

"I know what's been going on," I pretended. "So tell me what happened last night. She's my mother. I've a right to be told!"

Thabi shot me a sideways look and at last gave in. "Mehlokazulu decided to stop it once and for all," she whispered behind her hands. "He talked it through with your uncle, and they decided Kaqwelebana was for the chop." Now Thabi stopped, hands on hips. "I shouldn't be telling you this, Jabulani. You're far too young!"

"They were going to kill the Great Wife?" I said, not believing what I was hearing.

"Yes! Of course! It's a matter of honour, Jabulani. How could Mehlokazulu allow them to carry on like that? Sibongile too! I always thought she was a nice girl! Anyway, somehow Kaqwelebana and Mbopa got away. So did Mgobe and Sibongile. Perhaps Mehlokazulu didn't have the stomach to see it through. Now go away, and stop asking me questions!"

That same morning I was summoned to Mehlokazulu's hut. He explained to me what had happened. I played dumb, pretending what he said was news to me. It was obvious he was still boiling with anger.

"That woman has disgraced your father," he said. "And she'll pay a heavy price. But first we must find her."

I didn't have to ask Mehlokazulu to spell out what he meant by "*a heavy price*". His blood was up. His eyes were terrifyingly cold.

"I want you to come with me, and do some carrying," he said. "You're old enough now to be a proper *udibi*, and the experience will stand you in good stead. Gather together food and utensils. We'll leave at sun-up."

I held my head high as he spoke. Inside I was growing several inches. In spite of the reason for our expedition, it was still a great honour to know that Mehlokazulu thought I was now strong enough to keep pace with the warriors as they hunted or went into battle.

"Where are we going?" I asked.

"Away to the south. Along the river. And then across the white man's border into Natal. I expect they'll be hoping we won't come for them there."

I shivered. It felt unreal to be tracking down a member of the family. It was a kind of hunting I'd never expected. But this was a real adventure, promising danger and something quite new. Across the border! What was it like? Did the country out beyond the river in Natal look different to Zululand? Surely it must, or why would there be a "border" at all?

There were eight of us. I was there to look after Mehlokazulu and Nkubikazulu, and I padded along behind them, carrying what they needed. The others had to fend for themselves, including Shenkwana. He was a son of Sihayo too, though not by Kaqwelebana. Shenkwana made a great fuss about carrying his own pack. It obviously annoyed him that he had no *udibi* of his own to order about.

The weight on my back was heavy, and soon I began to worry that when it came to it, I'd struggle to keep up. Two sleeping mats, two cloaks, a couple of cooking pots, some cheese and a skin of beer: it seemed a light enough load when it was first tied on to me, but after a mile or so I was breathing heavily. I gritted my teeth, and concentrated hard on the rhythm of my walking, as if a drum was keeping my feet in time. It was a point of honour not to complain. I dreaded being found weak and wanting on my first day as a proper *udibi*.

As we marched, I wondered if things might have been different, had Sihayo not been at Ulundi with the King. I thought he might have calmed my brothers down, and made them think before they acted. Mercy was a word my father liked, and I was sure he'd have softened my brothers' desire for justice and revenge, even though he'd been so badly wronged. Did they have the right to fight on his behalf?

For there was no doubt, they were dressed to fight. All of my brothers are tall men, but the leopard skin bands tied around their heads with the snowy cow-tails drooping away on either side made them seem even taller and more impressive. Further cow tails decorated their upper arms and legs, and the monkey tails of their kilts made a bush of fur which swayed as they moved, making them look broader and sturdier than they really were. Each carried a war shield of bull's hide stretched tight across a frame, black with white patches. It would ward off any throwing spears that came their way, and in hand-to-hand combat could become a weapon itself, pushing and blocking from the left while the fearsome *iklwa*, the stabbing spear, was put to work from the right, thrusting into the enemy's heart.

Iklwa! It's a word that's beautiful and terrifying all at once, a word to say over and over to yourself, the very sucking sound the spear makes as the warrior withdraws its shaft from the body of a victim. It's a word to make enemies tremble, and Zulu warriors proud.

As if this wasn't enough, each man also carried an *iwisa*, a staff of iron-wood with a rounded end. An *iwisa* is far more than a stick because in the hands of Zulu warriors, this too can be the deadliest of weapons. A warrior will practise each day to be swift and precise in its use. The wood's as hard as a rock, and a single blow can finish a man.

On this occasion Mehlokazulu alone carried a rifle. He'd traded it with a white man at the mission station for a pile of cattle hides. He was a fair shot, but it wasn't his favoured weapon. He preferred his *iklwa*.

In the early afternoon we forded the *Mzinyathi*, the Buffalo River. It was winter, and there was no difficulty. If it had been during the rains, we'd have had to tie ourselves together and pull each other across. The dry and dusty far bank of the river marked the border, and the bare and scrubby dark-green hills which rose beyond it looked disappointingly the same as the ones I knew. I wanted marvels and mysteries. As we huddled together under our shields and cloaks for warmth that night, I hoped the hills wouldn't let me down.

The next morning we came to the hut of a border guard, a Zulu who had gone to work for the white men, a renegade. He eyed us suspiciously.

"Good morning, brother," said Mehlokazulu, with a lazy smile. "We're looking for two women, travelling with two men. Have you seen anything of them?"

"There's been no one this way," said the guard, but he dropped his eyes as he spoke. He was lying.

Mehlokazulu allowed himself a moment's silence, making the slightest of signs to the others with his right hand. They took a step or two forward.

"Now, let me ask you that question again," said Mehlokazulu. "The memory's a strange thing. It can play tricks, especially in one who spends so much time alone, as you obviously do."

The guard eyed us nervously. He made a great show of thinking hard. Then he said, as if he'd only just remembered it, "Come to think of it, I did see a woman and a man – just the one pair of strangers, though. Follow the river down, and you might still be lucky enough to find them."

Mehlokazulu thanked the guard with exaggerated politeness, and we moved on, tracing the river's course.

A little later, where the river bank was shallower and the tracks in the sand showed that animals regularly came to drink, Shenkwana stopped and lifted his head. "They've been here. I can smell the treachery," he said.

Suddenly I spotted two lonely figures just below the skyline.

"There!" I said, pointing ahead.

The lovers must have heard us, and turned where they stood on a little grassy ridge, a few hundred paces away. It was Mgobe with Sibongile, Sihayo's junior wife. They were holding hands. As she saw us, Sibongile fell to her knees and wrapped her head in her arms. Mgobe tried to pull her to her feet, to make her run, but in vain. She knew there was no escape.

When we'd crossed to where they stood, Mehlokazulu said nothing to Mgobe, not a word. He was left there on the little rise by the river all on his own, to think about his stupidity. Sibongile was tied at the wrists, and pulled along behind us for the rest of the afternoon, back the way we'd come.

I didn't see what happened to her, and I didn't ask. I hope the end was swift, for she was young and beautiful. The few words she'd ever spoken to me at the village had been gentle and kindly teasing.

Before Shenkwana took her away across the river, there'd been harsh words between the warriors about Sibongile's fate. The punishment for her crime was death, everyone agreed that. It was just a question of where and how. Mehlokazulu thought she should be taken home to kwaSihayo. The others thought there was nothing to be gained by that.

"Why waste food on her?" said Shenkwana evilly, and his opinion won the day. She was his aunt, and so the final vote went to him.

The last I saw of Sibongile, she was walking quietly and with a bowed head across the Buffalo River into Zululand at Shenkwana's side. When he returned to our camp later in the evening, Shenkwana came alone, a grim smile of satisfaction playing on his unpleasant face.

"Is it done?" asked Mehlokazulu quietly.

"Yes, brother. It is," came the smug reply.

At camp that night I was silent and a little frightened. Now the men talked about Kaqwelebana, and where she might be. Nkubikazulu was sure the border guard we'd met earlier knew more than he'd told.

"Let me go back and speak to him," he begged Mehlokazulu.

"You shouldn't go alone," said his brother.

"Then let's all go, and see whether we can jog his memory a little more," growled Nkubikazulu.

So the next morning, we found ourselves back at the border guard's hut. He wasn't pleased to see us, but not particularly surprised either. It seemed he'd sized up the situation, and decided to try a different line.

"I've heard," he said, coming close to Nkubikazulu's ear as if this was a great secret which had just that instant come to his attention, "that the other woman and man you're looking for may be making for Maziyana's *kraal*, about half a day's march up the valley. Only there's something you should know. Maziyana's not an easy man. Actually he's a very touchy fellow, and they're all well-armed up there. Most of them have guns and they know how to use them. If you're thinking of a raid, you need more than just the half dozen of you."

"Thank you brother," said Mehlokazulu smoothly, "and thank your informant. That's all very helpful. I'm sure what you've told us is right. It would be such a pity if it wasn't, wouldn't it?"

"Oh, you can depend on its truth," said the guard hurriedly.

"What shall we do?" hissed Nkubikazulu, when we were out of earshot. "Do you believe him?"

Mehlokazulu laughed throatily. "Don't you remember Maziyana?"

Nkubikazulu shook his head.

"He's one of our year group. We used to see a good deal of him once," said Mehlokazulu. "A good fighter, when he could be bothered! I fought him several times and lost as often as I won. You must remember him, brother! I wouldn't trust Maziyana further than I could see him. He never minded fighting dirty! And I seem to remember it was Mbopa who once told me he'd fallen out with his family, and gone south." He paused for a moment, then spat and spoke quickly, as if he'd made a decision. "We should listen to the guard's advice. Let's go prepared. I can still feel Maziyana's knee in my groin!"

It was agreed that Nkubikazulu would take Shenkwana to summon reinforcements from the *kraals* around kwaSihayo. Two days later we met them at the river crossing. There must have been a crowd 50 or so strong.

"You've done well," said Mehlokazulu, as my two brothers clasped hands. "Where did you find them all?"

"Nkubikazulu didn't need to ask twice," said a fellow I'd occasionally seen at our village but didn't know by name. "Kaqwelebana's had it coming a long time."

The men around him shouted and shook their spears in agreement.

27

"When do we strike?" said the first man, enthusiastically. "My blade's sharpened and ready. I hope there'll be a chance to use it!" I was surprised by the blood-lust. To hear the talk it was as if we were all out for a good day's deer hunting. I'd have died rather than show it, but I was scared at the thought of confronting this man Maziyana, with his straight shooting and his low cunning.

"We've not been idle," said Mehlokazulu, who'd been off scouting early that morning. "Two of us took a look at Maziyana's *kraal*, and it's not naturally well defended. There's no gorge, no nice safe caves like back home. Maziyana's huts are in the open. If we move upriver now, we can take them by surprise at dawn."

"But, what about the Great Wife? Is she there?" asked one of the warriors.

"She's there, all right," said Mehlokazulu with a grim smile. "She's found another hut to sit outside, and another village to order about."

I didn't sleep well that night, shivering and shifting from side to side under the cloak that covered me. It was very cold, and the stars danced and sparkled above us. They were still dancing when we rose next day. We were on the move before the sun was up.

As we approached Maziyana's *kraal*, half our warriors broke away and took up positions at the rear of the circle of huts. The rest of us simply ran without a sound to the front entrance and stood there, until on a signal from Mehlokazulu all the warriors sent up a great shout. At once people stumbled from the huts all around, rubbing the sleep from their eyes, astonished to see a crowd at their gates. For a few moments everyone stood and looked at everyone else.

"Where's Maziyana?" shouted Mehlokazulu, brandishing his shield and spear around his shoulders and head. A tallish man with an obvious squint elbowed his way brazenly forward to square up to him.

"You've found him!" said Maziyana. "Well, well, Mehlokazulu. After so long! Do you keep a stronger grip on your *iwisa* these days?"

"Strong enough, they tell me," said Mehlokazulu. "I like to stay in practice."

"And your father. Old man Sihayo. I hope he's well?" Maziyana smiled a lazy and insolent smile. "All things considered."

"Chief Sihayo has no quarrel with you," said Mehlokazulu.

"I should think he hasn't," said Maziyana with a leer. "Haven't I been looking after his property for

29

him? And very nicely too! She's proving very expensive to look after, you know!"

"If you're talking about Kaqwelebana, we've come to take her back," snapped Nkubikazulu. "And mind your tongue, warthog!"

In the background, I saw my mother emerge from a hut into the bright morning sunlight. Those around her took a step back so that she stood apart, a tree in her own space. Mbopa was nowhere to be seen. Kaqwelebana held herself high, and her face was like granite.

The words stung Maziyana, but he knew better than to argue, outnumbered as he was. He inclined his head towards Kaqwelebana. "You're welcome to *her*!" he hissed. "But understand this. Mbopa's a good friend. He comes to harm at your peril."

"He can do as he pleases," said Mehlokazulu, "Since his family ties mean so little to him! Just tell him never to show his face at kwaSihayo again."

"I'm sure he'll be devastated," said Maziyana with a sneer.

Hands made as if to push Kaqwelebana forward towards us, but she shrugged them off with a flick of her pudgy wrist. Sibongile might have looked frightened when she was captured, but the Great Wife was unrepentant. In a loud voice she asked Mehlokazulu what kind of a son he was to bring so many men to capture a mere woman, offering all kinds of insults to his manhood. Mehlokazulu ignored her, and gradually her shower of abuse fell away into a low muttering.

The rest of that terrible day was spent travelling uncomfortably back to the border. The skies had filled with cloud, and the weather was sticky and airless. I'd been so excited when we'd set out, but now the expedition had turned sour, and there was a weight in my heart. It was as if Kaqwelebana's dishonour had touched us all. No one talked, and finally even the Great Wife herself fell silent.

Once across the Buffalo River, the warriors said their goodbyes, but there was no rejoicing at a job well done. Their mood had changed.

Mehlokazulu spoke. "I'll remain with the Great Wife," he said meaningfully to the other brothers. "You go on to kwaSihayo. I shan't be far behind you."

They nodded their agreement gravely. I made as if to stay with Mehlokazulu, trying to be a good *udibi*.

As I hung back, he snapped at me, "You too, Jabulani. There's nothing more for you here."

It was my fault. I was beginning to learn that sometimes a warrior needs to be by himself.

31

Kaqwelebana deserved to die. This would be the hour of her death and it would be by Mehlokazulu's hands. Afterwards he'd need time and space to recover. When I stopped to think, I couldn't imagine what might be going on in his mind. To kill a mother!

When we'd set out five days previously I'd imagined a triumphant homecoming, with much feasting and beer drinking, but of course, it wasn't to be. Close to home, we passed Sipho on the path. "Sihayo's back from Ulundi!" he said. "What's happened? Tell me what's happened!"

A flicker of alarm crossed Nkubikazulu's face. I don't know whether anyone else noticed it, but I did.

My father was standing at the door of his hut as we entered the village. His arms were crossed, his face serious. Nkubikazulu broke off to pay his respects, and tell him that Mehlokazulu would shortly also return.

Later I was there when my two brothers told Sihayo what had happened, simply and truthfully. My father let them finish.

"It seems to me," he said finally, speaking slowly in his deep voice, "that this was well done and badly done. I suppose the fate of the women was inevitable and deserved, though I must say I'd have liked a say in the matter..."

"We didn't know when you'd be back from Ulundi," Nkubikazulu butted in, rather sulkily. A glance from Sihayo silenced him. They'd had their chance to speak.

"...As I said, I'd have liked a say, but only because you're young men, and go about things as young men do. Old age brings experience, you see, and there are things you don't yet understand.

"On the other hand, I'm sure this will bring trouble. The white men, with whom we trade and with whom we should share respect, are divided. When they see a Zulu, some of them see only a threat. They're looking for an excuse to teach us a lesson, to put us in our place. They want us to know they are the masters. This is exactly what I've been talking about with King Cetshwayo. Unfortunately, by crossing the border and acting as you have, you've probably given them the excuse they seek."

Mehlokazulu was on the defensive now. "The Great Wife met her end on Zulu soil," he said. "And so did Sibongile. We took great care with that!"

"It won't make a scrap of difference," said Sihayo, shaking his head. "If they want to, the white men will say this was a declaration of war. An invasion."

Nkubikazulu looked genuinely puzzled. Mehlokazulu hung his head. He'd so much wanted my father's approval, and in trying to do what he'd thought was for the best, he'd failed.

"Where did you bury her, Mehlokazulu?" said my father quietly. "I should like a little time there alone." There was a pause, and then he added, "She was so beautiful, long ago, when we were both young..."

Six full months passed by between then and the theft of the cattle from Skull Hill, back where my story began. That's a great number of days in the hot sun hoeing or carrying water, or in my case, chasing cows around the thorn bushes. It's plenty of time to forget wise words. But though he wasn't the cleverest man in the village, and though he'd been stung to have been rebuked by his father, Nkubikazulu had listened closely to what Sihayo said.

Remember, when the cattle were stolen from under my nose, Mehlokazulu and Sihayo were with King Cetshwayo at Ulundi. Now Nkubikazulu sent out scouts to see if they could discover where the cattle had been taken. They reported back that there was a great camp of white men just the far side of the *Mzinyathi* River, but beyond where I'd been able to see. There were many carts and oxen there, and possibly thousands of men, though it was hard to be sure, so far did the line of wagons stretch. The scouts also said they'd seen strange carts with huge cylinders of iron on their backs. They were puzzled and suggested that maybe the British carried the bones of their ancestors into battle with them for protection. I'd seen pictures of these wagons in the books at the mission station, and knew what they were. Full of myself, I told Nkubikazulu that the British white men called them "cannons", and that they were like guns, but many, many times more powerful.

He said with a sly smile that, yes, he too had heard that when white men went to war they used machines to help them fight. They needed such help he said, because they were so weak compared with Zulu warriors. But what use were wagons? They'd just get stuck in the mud, and they weren't going to frighten him, he laughed. Personally he couldn't wait to get to grips with the white warriors and show them who had the greater power.

I asked Nkubikazulu again why he thought the British white men had come.

"I don't understand what they want with us," I said. "What harm have we ever done them?"

Sometimes Nkubikazulu treated me as if I was too far beneath him to bother with. This time, he humoured me.

"Well, what our father Sihayo has told me is this. Because of what we did to protect his honour at Maziyana's *kraal*, the white man's Queen demands that your father, Mehlokazulu and myself should be handed over for punishment."

"*Ay-ih*," I sighed.

"And the White Queen's ministers also demand that we should give them 500 head of cattle, and much else besides. They've even said we must put away our spears and never assemble at Ulundi to train as an army as we do each year at the *Great Umkhosi* festival. They have said we must agree now or accept the consequences."

"And what does King Cetshwayo say?" I asked.

"He loves your father as if he were his own son," said Nkubikazulu with pride. "And he has said he will never allow it. He would rather die first."

In the hours that followed, Nkubikazulu sent for men from the country around kwaSihayo to come and help, particularly any who had rifles. He ordered them and our own warriors into the caves that surrounded the entrance to the gorge which led from the

Mzinyathi River up to kwaSihayo. If we were attacked they'd try to ambush the white men there. No one was to stray far from home, and the women and children were told that at the first sign of trouble they were to disappear into the bush or hide in caves slightly further away where they could be safe. Every single cow and ox that we owned was rounded up, and brought inside the *kraal*.

Very early the next morning we were woken in our huts. The scouts had reported that the white men were on the march. They could be near kwaSihayo in no time at all. I talked to Sipho.

"What should we do?" he said.

"I don't want to run away with the children and hide in a cave," I said. "I want to go up to the gorge to help."

We found Nkubikazulu, who was heading off to supervise the preparations.

"All right," he said, and looked hard at me. "But there may be many of them and few of us. If things go badly, the most useful job you can do is to make sure you escape and take news of what's happened to your father and to the King. Do you understand? Will you promise me?"

I looked him in the eye and made my promise. Until

that day, I'd never been sure about Nkubikazulu, for all that he was my brother. Unlike Mehlokazulu he could be moody and difficult, but out of the shadow of his father and elder brother, he seemed to grow in stature.

Nkubikazulu had turned to go, but suddenly he stopped and spun on his heels. "Of course what you could do now would be to drive the cattle into the gorge..."

"I thought they'd been brought into the *kraal* for safety," said Sipho, puzzled.

Nkubikazulu's reply was unexpectedly harsh. "Learn one thing. Never question an order in a time of war," he snapped. Sipho jumped as if he'd been stung by a wasp. "Just do as you're told!" And Nkubikazulu stomped off up the valley ahead of us.

We got behind the cattle and with our backs to Sihayo's hut drove them out and up into the end of the gorge nearest the village. They protested loudly at being sent on what seemed to them a wrong path. Eventually they dug in their heels and refused to move any further forward, however hard we beat their backsides. It was soaking wet inside the gorge because of the unusually heavy summer rains. The sun only shone there for an hour or so each day and the damp rocks underfoot were very slippery and dangerous.

Now I understood Nkubikazulu's thinking. The gorge would be blocked by a seething mass of animal flesh. If the red soldiers came that way, they'd find it hard to make progress. A whistle came from above us. It was Nkubikazulu.

"That's good," he shouted. "That's very good. Now come up here where you'll be safe. Quickly!" We climbed up the side of the gorge by a narrow path to a spur of rock halfway up the cliff face. Nkubikazulu pushed us into the jaws of a cave at the back of the ledge.

"Excellent work!" he said. "Let's see what the white man makes of that!"

I caught a flash of red as the British soldiers appeared at the river end of the gorge and started to climb towards the village. They saw the cattle, and hesitated. They didn't see our warriors hidden in the rocks high to each side of them. At a sign from Nkubikazulu, when the red soldiers had climbed almost level with the cattle that reared and turned in front of them, our men started to roll heavy rocks down from the cliffs. The rocks bounced unpredictably on the sides of the canyon, crashing into the line of red soldiers. I saw one of them stumble and fall trying to avoid the path of a massive boulder.

Another collapsed lifeless to the ground, struck a glancing blow by a lump of granite. The soldiers looked from side to side in alarm, not sure what was happening. Then seconds later they found that Zulus as well as white men own rifles, and scrambled for cover as shots ricocheted down on to the floor of the gorge. Now they were within range of a well-aimed spear too.

There was screaming and shouting from both Zulus and white men in the confusion, and for a few moments I thought the red soldiers would simply turn and run. But they gathered themselves, stood their ground and began to return fire. Bullets echoed around the canyon walls. I saw several Zulus fall, mortally wounded. Compared to the white men, our shooting was wild and wide of the mark.

Sipho shrank back into the cave. He was shaking with fear, and I felt uncertain and panicky myself, torn between keeping open our way of escape and hiding in the dark.

I watched as Nkubikazulu died. He stood up on the outcrop of rock and aimed his rifle down at a pair of red soldiers who were half hidden by a boulder on the canyon floor to our left. I didn't hear the shot that killed him because of the general noise, but I saw his body jerk back with the bullet's impact. He doubled up and fell awkwardly across the stony platform where he stood.

I slithered my way across the dirt like a snake to where Nkubikazulu lay. He was still alive, but only just.

"Go now!" he croaked. "Remember your promise. Find the King, and tell him..." He swallowed hard, and his eyes were closing. Nkubikazulu made one last great effort. "...Tell him to avenge what happened today!" And with that his chest heaved for one final time.

My brother Nkubikazulu died the best death a Zulu warrior can imagine, bravely defending his home and family. For this he will be remembered and praised for generations to come. But that day, the effect on our fighters of seeing their leader struck down was devastating. They began to fall back along the edges of the canyon towards the village, and as they did so the cattle began to follow them along the floor, opening a path for the red soldiers to force their way up the gorge.

Crawling back into the cave on my hands and knees, I begged Sipho to come out of the darkness.

"I must go," I implored, laying hands on him to drag him towards the entrance. "I've promised my brother. Come with me, please, Sipho. There's no time to lose!"

My impatience nearly cost us our lives. We waited until what we thought was a good moment, and then when the great mass of attacking red soldiers surged past us up the canyon, Sipho and I picked our route on up the cliff face, to make good our escape through the fields at the top. I remember that as I climbed, I caught sight of black men wearing red bandanas and torn white trousers streaming on behind the red soldiers, supporting their attack. They didn't look like Zulus, but in the panic I couldn't be sure. I wondered what any black men were doing in the white man's army.

We were so lucky. As we pulled ourselves up the last few feet, scrabbling for a hold on the loose shale at the cliff's top, a shout came from below and bullets whistled through the air, pinging off the crag to either side of us.

We ran on up to a viewpoint where we knew the roofs of kwaSihayo would be just visible in the distance. Sipho was there just before me, and his "*Ay-ih*" told me all I needed to know. Several columns of dirty smoke were rising high into the sky, and at the base of the smoke we could see tongues of flame, as the thatched sides and roofs of our home burned. In a few minutes more kwaSihayo would be a few piles of charred wood and ash. The white man's army had come to the land of the Zulus.

The two of us had very different things on our minds. Sipho's eyes were fixed on the burning village. He was terribly afraid for his brothers, sisters and parents. All I could think of was my promise to Nkubikazulu to take news to the King. I feared the journey, but even more I feared travelling alone.

I took Sipho by the shoulders, and turned him away from the smoke and flames, making him look at me.

"Listen to me," I said urgently. "We've got to keep moving."

"I can't leave my family," he said tearfully. "Not now!"

"They'll be safely holed up in one of the caves," I tried. I knew I didn't sound convincing.

"It's no good," he said desperately. "You go on. I'll stay."

"Please come with me," I begged him, almost on my knees. "You'll certainly be in danger here. The red soldiers may do anything. Perhaps they'll put a guard on the village. Perhaps they're hoping to draw us into a bigger battle. I've lost one brother already today. I don't want to lose my best friend as well. And you'll be more use to me on the journey than you can ever be here." I added weakly, "I don't think I can do this on my own."

"Do you really think they'll be safe?" he asked, wavering.

"I'm sure of it," I lied. "Now, come *on*!"

Reluctantly, and looking over his shoulder every few yards, Sipho did as I asked.

Neither of us had even been to Ulundi, and the King's quarters were far away to the east. I'd heard my brothers say a man could make it on foot comfortably in two days. My father had even boasted that on one occasion when he was young and much slimmer than he was now, he'd left home before dawn and arrived after midnight. Even at the time the half-smiles on the faces of the circle of listeners had made me doubt the truth of the tale.

But we were tired after the events of the day, in our heads as well as our bodies, and the further we went the less we knew the way. People eyed us suspiciously. Perhaps they thought we were runaways.

"Who are you? And why are *you* going to Ulundi?" we were asked more than once, from behind narrowed eyes. When we answered that the white men had overwhelmed kwaSihayo, there was shocked surprise and more questions, but offers of food and shelter too.

Finally, on the third afternoon, footsore and burned by the sun, our legs scarred by the prickles of a thousand thorn bushes, we perched high on a hillside and took in the size and grandeur of King Cetshwayo's royal *kraals* where they lay in the plain of Ulundi.

"*Ay-ih*," said Sipho. "Look at those huts. I never knew there were so many Zulus!"

There were hundreds and hundreds of huts large and small stretching across the dusty plain, and the dots of people everywhere. For the first time in my life I felt just a mere country boy, overawed by the size and scale of royal Ulundi. There were boys like us driving cattle, women coming back from the fields laden with food and reeds, warriors exercising, children playing, chasing each other and throwing sticks. Everywhere we looked there was activity. I thought of ants scurrying busily around an ant hill. The horror we'd left behind us seemed to belong to a completely different world.

We came to the gate. Two of the tallest Zulus I'd ever seen stood by it, unsmiling and severe. Though we were a spear's distance from them, they pretended not to notice us.

Despite my fatigue, I stood as tall as I could and said, "We've come to see Chief Sihayo, brothers. Can you tell us where we can find him?"

Not a muscle twitched in response. For a moment I thought they were going to ignore us completely, and I began to feel panic rise inside me. Had Sipho and I come so far for nothing? Then one of the warriors turned his wary hawk's eye on us and looked us over very, very slowly, up and down, up and down.

Finally a thumb jerked towards the centre of the huge open space behind him, and the warrior lifted his eyes to scour the horizon again. Not a word was said. Sipho and I looked at each other, and scurried between the guards in the direction of the thumb.

Twice more we asked for my father's whereabouts before, walking a few hundred paces to the far side of the *kraal* where we guessed the King's own hut would be, we finally saw a familiar broad back, and heard lively conversation in a deep voice, accompanied by dancing hands. Chief Sihayo was doing what he liked best, entertaining a group of listening admirers.

We hovered a few feet away until suddenly, aware that he was no longer commanding the full attention of his audience, my father swivelled, shading his eyes against the low sun. I rushed forward and fell at his knees.

"*Nkosi*!" I said simply, showing him my greatest respect. He pulled me to my feet.

"This can't be good news," he said softly. "Not for you to have journeyed all this way. What is it, young Jabulani? And you Sipho! What is it? Tell me quickly!"

My words came in a rush. I told him everything that

46

had happened. When he heard about Nkubikazulu, my father Sihayo put his hands to his head as if trying to shut out the words. He was still dazed, wandering around in a small circle, when Mehlokazulu ran up to us.

"Jabulani!" he said, laughing. "Have you run away to join the army then, little brother?" But even as he spoke, his words died on his lips, as he saw his father's grief.

"It's Nkubikazulu," I blurted out. "Your brother's dead."

Mehlokazulu was inconsolable. He hurled himself to the ground, wailing and banging his arms and body on the rock-hard surface. Then his sadness turned to anger, and he vowed a bloody vengeance against those who had taken Nkubikazulu's life, his steely words echoing around the dusty bowl where we stood.

That night I slept as soundly as I've ever done, falling into blackness away from a throbbing head and aching limbs. The sun was already high in the sky when Sipho prodded me awake.

"We're to see the King," he said excitedly.

"Is he coming to visit then?" I murmured, still half asleep and unsure for a moment where I was.

"No, stupid! This is Ulundi. Remember? We're summoned to meet him. He wants to hear what happened from our own lips! Get up, and make yourself ready! Come on."

I dragged my aching legs to the river and splashed water on my face, trying to make myself as alert as I could for the King.

At the door to his quarters we were met by a solemn dignified man with grey hair and stooped shoulders. My father introduced him as Themba, and said with a warm smile that he was one of the King's closest and most trusted attendants. Much later I was to find out that Themba wasn't nearly as old and slow as he seemed.

Themba reminded Sipho and me that as custom required we should crawl into the King's presence on our hands and knees, deliberately keeping our eyes down and away from the stool on which the King sat in the cool shadows.

King Cetshwayo's voice was firm and resonant. "Get up, little warriors," he said. "I want to have a good look at you."

We stood. The King was a big man, and powerfully built, his shoulders broad under his leopard-skin cape. His well-oiled skin glistened in the light which shafted in from the side of the hut. It might have been a king's dwelling, and so larger and more airy than ours, but I was surprised to see no greater finery inside than in my father's hut back home. The skins and furs which were cast around the floor and across the chairs were certainly of the best quality, but there was nothing else which would have told a visitor that he was in the presence of royalty. Only the pair of giant ivory tusks arching across behind King Cetshwayo's seat were out of the ordinary.

The King listened gravely as we told him of the white men's arrival, and laughed at the thought of the cattle which had blocked their attack. He shook his head when he heard about Nkubikazulu's death, and asked careful questions about the red soldiers. How many had we seen? What arms had they carried? What was their spirit like? Had they looked scared? Or confident? Eventually his questions dried up, and there was a moment's silence. Then he spoke again, his eyes blazing.

"Well done, Jabulani! And you, Sipho! Sometimes an old man like me fears for the future of his people. We begin to think that things were better in the old days, that warriors were braver and stronger then, that no one cares for the Zulu traditions of honour now as they used to. But if all our young men are like you boys, what do we need to fear? Isn't that right Sihayo, old friend?"

"Jabulani is my son, your majesty," said Sihayo. "So it isn't for me to say. But Sipho certainly seems a fine young man."

"Jabulani is indeed your son!" laughed the King. "A shoot from the same tree. And it may even prove stronger than the old wood. I hope we shall see more of you both, young Jabulani and Sipho."

Suddenly he became serious again. "So the question is, what shall we do next?" He paused dramatically, and spoke to my father. "I must think, and talk with my ancestors, then consult you and my other trusted counsellors, Sihayo. Only then will it be the time for action."

He turned one last time to me. "Don't worry, Jabulani, your brother won't be forgotten! He was a brave and worthy warrior, as you will be, and we shall sing his praises often." And with a wave of his hand, we were dismissed.

It was the time of the Royal Festival, the *Great Umkhosi*. Every year men from each Zulu regiment arrived at Ulundi to sing the praises of their King and to learn to fight together. Each small article of uniform, every feather and wrist-band, was trimmed and cleaned. Every warrior wanted to show their prowess in front of their friends – to be the best he could be. New dances and songs were learned and performed, the King's fields were hoed, his fences mended, and so the Zulu nation was kept ready for action. It's part of the year's round. Ever since I can remember, our family and friends have gathered at the gate of kwaSihayo to sing those taking part in the *Great Umkhosi* on their way to Ulundi.

But this year the celebrations had changed into something more serious. Rumours had started to filter into Ulundi weeks beforehand that the British soldiers were preparing for battle.

"The British know the King will never give them what they want," said Mehlokazulu that afternoon. He was breathing heavily, his hands on his knees. He'd found a low, dusty hill outside the *kraal*'s perimeter fence, and he made himself run up and down it each day, pumping his legs through the yielding, muscle-stretching sand. "The British just want an excuse to fight. They think that a single battle will crush the Zulu spirit."

A mighty Zulu army had been slowly forming at Ulundi for the first time in 25 years. Every day, from every wind, more and more warriors had been trooping into camp accompanied by their *udibi* and followed by a straggle of women and girls carrying food and beer on their heads. Every day more and more temporary grass huts had filled the spaces on the plain.

"Will the British come even here?" I asked, hoping the answer might be no.

"They will if we don't stop them," said Mehlokazulu bullishly. "And it won't be easy, you know. King Cetshwayo always thought they might attack from the coast, near Eshowe. Now your father says there are two or three different columns of red soldiers advancing from different directions."

He straightened himself, and eyed the hill, ready for another assault on its summit. "Don't look so worried, Jabulani! Keep yourself fit, like me. It'll take your mind off things!"

That night, as every night, while the huge orange disc of the sun sank into the bed of the misty grey and purple hills, a great fire was lit in the great space before the King's palace. Around its flames, thousands of us ate strips of dried beef, cakes of mealie-meal and sweet potatoes. Teams of warriors from the different regiments, dressed in their own distinctive finery, danced and shouted the praises of their ancestors, each trying to outdo the other in skill. Sipho and I sat and dreamed of the day in years to come when we and all the boys of our year group would be gathered together to make up our own new regiment. Then we'd be out there showing off alongside Mehlokazulu.

"I wonder what our regiment'll be called?" said Sipho idly.

"We might be 'The Eagles'," I answered. "Think of the speed to the kill, and the strength in the claws."

"Or 'The Wasps'," he said, trying to go one better. "Hard to catch and stinging the enemy to death."

"Wasn't there a regiment called that? Back in Shaka Zulu's time?"

"Don't know," said Sipho. "But really I'd like to have been born with Mehlokazulu and Nkubikazulu, and become an *inGobamakhosi*. They're the best."

"It's just not much of a name," I said. *InGobamakhosi* or "Bender of Kings" had never seemed an impressive title to me.

We were watching a troop of *inGobamakhosi* preparing to dance. There was Mehlokazulu, standing to one side, tall and proud. It brought a lump to my throat, thinking of my other brother, now dead, who if things had been different might have been dancing too.

The *inGobamakhosi* made the earth shake with the pounding of their feet on the baked earth. Their cowtails made swirls of white in the firelight. Before the warriors hovered Sigwelewele, the regiment's commander, urging them on, his great head thrust forward, his shoulders swaying. Their hoarse shouts rang out and echoed across the plain above the hubbub of the crowd, as the sweat glistened on their foreheads and chests. Mehlokazulu had his moment, as one of Sigwelewele's lieutenants, surging to the front and shouting the story of our family, the battles our ancestors had fought, their bravery and feats of strength. At the climax of his song he yelled a chorus of praise to Nkubikazulu, and to his glorious death, protecting his home and family. From all sides came a roar of approval, the women shrieking their agreement into the skies.

I don't know quite how the trouble started. I think a lot of beer had been drunk by this time in the evening, and tongues were getting loose. The *uThulwana*, the "dust raisers", had taken over the dance, when suddenly we saw that some of the *inGobamakhosi* who'd stayed at the front of the crowd were staring down the *uThulwana* as they strutted and preened in front of the watchers. The *uThulwana*, who were older men, clearly didn't like the attention and the clever comments they were getting from the younger warriors. Suddenly they broke off from their display. Tempers flared and men from each regiment began to threaten the other with their sticks.

Around us the women in the crowd were cackling their amusement. They were urging the two sides on, daring them to strike the first blow.

"What's going on?" I asked Sipho.

"I don't know," Sipho said, "but it's all good fun."

"It's about girls, of course," shouted a boy who was standing beside us. "A few years ago, the King kept the *uThulwana* waiting before he allowed them to marry. Then they stole some of the girls the *inGobamakhosi* always assumed would be theirs because they were the same age, and far too young for the *uThulwana*. Now every time the two regiments meet, it's the same. One or two songs, too much beer, and something sets them off. The *inGobamakhosi* call out 'cradle-snatchers', or the *uThulwana* mention 'little boys', and that's it!"

"But they're about to go to battle," I said. "How can they fight each other one day, and the enemy the next?"

"It's not that serious!" the boy laughed. "It's happened before, and I expect it'll happen again. They're just getting in the mood for the red soldiers!"

But beyond the fire I could see that eyes were blazing. Tempers had been lost. Now spears were being waved in the faces of the other regiment. It looked as if at any moment someone would be seriously hurt or killed. Then to one side the crowd suddenly fell respectfully quiet. Through them strode the imposing figure of the King, resplendent in leopard skin, trailing feathers of every bird known to man. The warriors were still trading insults backwards and forwards but one by one they sank back, and silence slowly settled on them too. The King waited until every last man felt his powerful presence. He said nothing, but searched the eyes of each one coldly, his brow furrowed and his arms folded, as if he expected better of his warriors. Then he turned on his heel and stalked off back to his hut.

In the morning, I left Sipho and went to wait on Mehlokazulu. It seemed that any bad blood there'd been the previous evening had been completely forgotten. There was a sense of purpose around the camp. It was thronged with people about their business, and warriors of different regiments were mingling without a second thought.

I brought Mehlokazulu porridge and fresh water, and tidied his sleeping mat. His face was grim as he sharpened his spear, the stone making a zip-ZIP sound as it slid rhythmically up and down the blade.

"What's happening, Mehlokazulu? Is Ulundi like this every morning?" I said, trying to make conversation, as I tied the mat into a bundle.

His face creased into a smile. "Not quite the same as sleepy kwaSihayo is it, little brother?"

"Are you good friends with the *uThulwana* again?" I asked.

"Oh, that?" Mehlokazulu seemed unconcerned. "That was nothing. Just a little stirring of the warriors' blood!" He laughed, then suddenly became more animated. "You know, you've arrived in Ulundi at a very remarkable moment. Perhaps it was meant to be! Today will be a day like no other. Today the Zulu army, the *impi*, will make ready for battle. You should come and watch. See what has to be done for warriors who look death in the eye!"

"I don't want you to die," I said in a small voice, suddenly very afraid for the older brother I worshipped. In my head I relived the moment Nkubikazulu had fallen. I saw his last movements, heard his last words.

Mehlokazulu stopped sharpening his spear, and turned to face me.

"Death reaches out to all of us in the end," he said, matter-of-factly. "How would you rather end your days, on the battlefield, or from a snake bite? By a spear or with a fever?"

"It frightens me," I said frankly. "*I* don't want to die at all."

"Of course you don't. Death scares me too," he said. "But death is only a moment. A warrior who has no fear is a burden in battle. He will be reckless, and endanger his brother warriors. We need all the help we can get, from the *sangomas*, from our ancestors, from the power deep inside us. We need to become supple of arm, and strong of soul, to control our fear."

Mehlokazulu's words were confident, and the sound of his voice was comforting. I felt his courage pour into me. He took me by the shoulders.

"Come on," he said, standing and weighing his spear in his hand. "This should be a special occasion. A privilege! Something to tell your children. Thank your brother Nkubikazulu in the quietness of your heart. Without his death you wouldn't be here to see this!"

It was all I could do to choke back a tear.

At Nodwengu, the parade ground which stretched out on the southern edge of Ulundi, the light was so bright it hurt, and the clamour of our army was deafening. I blinked, and rubbed my eyes against the brilliance of the sky and the reflected gleam from countless spears and shields. Thousands of warriors were milling around expectantly until, on the sound of a horn, the regiments separated from each other like fat on boiling water, and we turned to face the King. From my position at Mehlokazulu's side, I saw Themba step forward. He placed a seat where the ground was a little higher, so that the King could see everyone, and everyone could see him.

Softly at first, and then with increasing volume, a rhythmic humming rose from the lips of the *impi* and seemed to hover in the dry, dusty air, as if we were surrounded by swarms of bees, not ranks of soldiers. It was a sound that sent a thrill through me from my stomach to my scalp. I shuddered.

From where we stood at the rear of the *inGobamakhosi*, I had to crane my neck to catch sight of what went on, dodging from side to side for a clear view round the warriors' broad shoulders.

In the centre of the parade ground danced a band of *sangomas*, singing their songs of magic to the air and the ancestors. In their hands they carried bowls, containing a liquid they were very careful not to spill by their dancing.

Mehlokazulu became aware that I was struggling to see. "Go through to the front," he said, and I slipped around the side of the regiment away from him.

From my new position, I could see a freshly dug pit near the dancing medicine men, not very wide, but maybe a man's height in depth.

Regiment by regiment, in groups of three or four, the men approached the pit. Each went forward to a *sangoma* who poured a few drops of the liquid from one of the bowls into the warriors' outstretched hands. The men drank it down, and then after a few seconds, one by one retched into the pit in front of them.

"It's powerful medicine," whispered the soldier at whose side I stood, mesmerized. "It protects, and cleans the body of the warrior from all impurities. One day, when you're a man, you too may share in it."

I watched as Mehlokazulu and the other *inGobamakhosi* in their turn took the medicine. As he drank, Mehlokazulu's face was creased by lines of concentration, his eyes set dark and serious. He held himself tall and rigid at the sacred moment. Even from 30 or more paces away, I could sense the power that welled up from deep inside the *sangomas*. The circle of ground around them seemed to shimmer and hum. My head buzzed and throbbed as if I had a touch of the sun.

I couldn't tell you whether I stood by the pit a moment or half a day. I was spellbound by the ceremony, repeated over and over again for every man in the King's army. When I finally turned to seek out Mehlokazulu, my feet seemed to skim the ground rather than walk, and the ache in my limbs after our long journey seemed to have completely disappeared.

Mehlokazulu pointed and I saw to our right that a huge black bull had been corralled into an enclosed area. It was a magnificent beast, its coat sleek and shining in the bright sun. It had carried itself with the nobility of a king among animals, but it was being run to the point of exhaustion by the warriors. Its legs were becoming unsteadier by the minute.

"Will they kill it?" I asked Mehlokazulu.

"Its strength will become our strength," he answered. His eyes were distant, glazed, caught up in the power of the ceremony.

Suddenly Sipho was at my side. "I've been looking for you everywhere!" he said crossly, and for a moment I felt guilty that I'd not given him a second thought all morning. "Why didn't you wait for me?"

"Look at them go," I said, trying to distract him. The warriors were chasing the bull from side to side of the corral, and then, as it became confused and sank to its knees, a larger number of men moved forward with mighty shouts and seized it.

"*Ay-ih*," exclaimed Sipho. "Rather them than me!"

Showing enormous strength and courage, fired by the medicine, they wrestled the animal off its feet, twisting its vicious horns from side to side until its neck was finally broken. A great cry went up from all sides, and there was an explosion of singing from around us.

Other *inGobamakhosi* had begun to build a fire, heaving the bull on to a platform above it to cook. Mehlokazulu supervised the work. Nobody wanted anything of us, so Sipho and I wandered away.

"Has Mehlokazulu told you?" Sipho said, as we strolled around the edge of the parade ground.

"Told me what?" I asked uncertainly.

"They're sending us home."

"Oh," I replied. And then after a pause, "Why?"

"A party of women is going back near kwaSihayo tomorrow, under escort. I asked if we could go too, and it was agreed."

I tried hard to draw on the power of the morning's ceremony to overcome my disappointment, but it was no use. I turned and snapped, "How could you, Sipho? I'm surprised at you." I was angry and felt a little betrayed. I wanted to be a part of what I'd just seen, and I didn't want it taken away by Sipho. "Do what you want, but never, ever answer for me," I said crossly. "If being safe's what you're after, it may be safer here than at home. Anyway..."

I stopped midstream, because suddenly it was clear to me what I was going to do, and Sipho had no part in it. I couldn't leave Mehlokazulu now. If the *impi* was going into battle, I'd go with them. Sipho would have to do as he thought fit.

"Anyway what?" he said in a sulk.

"Oh, nothing," I said, disguising my thoughts. "Perhaps you're right. You want to know what's become of your family. It's only fair. You came with me against your will. Thank you for that, at least, Sipho. I have no right to tell you what you ought to do."

We wandered back to watch the activity around the fire in a truce of silence. When the bull's flesh was cooked, Sigwelewele and Mehlokazulu took slices of it and threw them to the warriors. Each took a mouthful of the meat, then threw the strip into the air for the next man to catch. Each catch was accompanied by a shout from the warriors. The better the catch, the louder the cheer.

Late in the afternoon, I made my way back to my

father Sihayo's hut. As luck would have it, he was there alone. I threw myself on the ground before him in obedience, and told him what Sipho had said. I asked if it was true.

"Sipho seemed delighted with the idea," he said. "Don't you want to accompany your friend back to see kwaSihayo again?"

"There may be nothing left of our home," I answered.

"Even if the huts are all burned and the cattle stolen, the land will still be there," Sihayo said seriously.

My father was making it clear he thought I should go with Sipho, and in his presence my nerve was weakening. Before it failed me completely, I took a deep breath and launched into my speech.

"Isn't there some use for me with the *impi* as it goes to fight for our freedom? I'd do anything, you know. I'll carry Mehlokazulu's spears and sleeping mat. I can scout for the warriors. Who will suspect a boy wandering on the hillsides of doing anything more than guarding cattle? I can spy on the white men and bring information. I'm as quick and silent as anyone. Haven't I proved my courage and endurance in coming here? I'd rather die with honour, my father, than be sent away with the women."

I fell silent after this outburst. I kept my eyes down, afraid I'd see anger if I met his gaze.

There was a pause, and then I felt his hands on my head, raising my face so that he could look at me.

"Is this really what you want?" he asked. "Are you sure?"

I nodded.

"Then we'll see what Mehlokazulu says. If he agrees I'll mention it to the King himself when we talk tonight. Come back and see me in the morning."

While Sipho snored his head off that night, I scarcely slept at all, thinking about what I had said, and what might happen to me tomorrow.

I was part of the great Zulu *impi* as it marched out of Ulundi, first to the south and then to the west. As we went, I could hear the warriors muttering scornfully about the white men and their wicked ways. Before we'd marched out of Nodwengu's gates, the King had spoken to his soldiers.

"The British white men could be our friends," he said gravely. "But they have chosen to be our enemies. They have begun to ravage our land, to burn our houses, to seize our cattle. And why? Because they say we should have asked *them* before we administered justice to criminals. Because they do not approve of our marriage customs. Do we need to ask the white man's approval?"

A great shout of anger rose from the army spread in front of him.

"Very well. Go then and fight for your freedom. Fight for your way of life. And by your strength of body and spirit, let us restore our friendship with the white man."

That first night the army settled itself down by the great Mfolozi River. Below the banks of white sand there was now just a trickle of dirty water. The gouge the river had taken from the plain told its story. At one moment it could be a peaceful stream, and then after rain, within minutes, a violent torrent. Mehlokazulu paced up and down the banks, fretting and fussing.

"What's the matter, brother?" I asked.

"I can't believe it," he said, casting an arm up the flat valley where we camped. As far as the eye could see there were Zulu soldiers lighting fires, preparing meals, telling stories to each other to keep up their courage. "This is all my fault. Why didn't we just let Kaqwelebana go her own stupid way? It would have been far better."

"Nonsense," said a voice, booming from the twilight. Its power and closeness made me jump. Behind us stood Sigwelewele, the commander of the *inGobamakhosi*.

"Nonsense! And you should know better than to allow your weak thoughts to infect your little brother, Mehlokazulu. The truth is that the white men are greedy. For a long time now, they've wanted our land, though they have plenty of their own. They think because they have more guns than us, that we'll roll

67

over and let our bellies be tickled like the dogs of which they're so peculiarly fond."

"But, Sigwelewele," sighed Mehlokazulu, "if you're up against a herd of rhinoceros who want to stampede through your pumpkin field, what do you do? Throw your spears at them and risk being killed? Or do you tease them and bribe them and try to divert them round the edge and away from your crops. We should be talking, not going to war."

"Listen!" said the commander. "It's been tried. King Cetshwayo himself told me that he's twice held peace-talks with the white men, and twice they've sent him away empty-handed as if he were a small boy asking for fruit from their orchard. He says he feels as if he's trying to avoid a falling tree. Trying, and failing!"

"I didn't know that," said Mehlokazulu, still unconvinced.

"Anyway, I didn't come to talk to you about plans for peace," said Sigwelewele, crashing on. "But about plans for fighting. You're one of the people I rely on, you know that, Mehlokazulu. Whatever happens, we're going to need discipline among the warriors, and I know your men listen to you. If it comes to a full-scale battle, as we all expect it will, maybe in six days' time, after the new moon, the *inGobamakhosi* will form the front part of the left horn. Tshingwayo wants his youngest and fittest men there. This is going to require cool heads."

Tshingwayo was King Cetshwayo's appointed commander-in-chief, a grey-haired man in his sixties, a master in battle, so everyone said. The King's final words as he'd sent us off from Nodwengu were to obey Tshingwayo as if he were the King himself.

Ever since the time of Shaka Zulu, the greatest King of them all, the founder of our nation, the scourge of our enemies, mover of mountains, the Zulu army has divided itself into horns, chest and loins, a living picture of the cattle who bring us life. It's the first thing I ever learned about being a Zulu warrior.

When we were younger, Sipho and I had played every day at being Zulu armies, imagining ourselves, like Sigwelewele, as commanders of regiments, and making lightning attacks on the girls hoeing in the fields.

"You be the right horn and I'll be the left," he would whisper, as we crouched behind a bush, planning our raid.

The Zulu idea of battle is this. First of all, the "chest" of the army shows itself to the enemy head on.

The "chest" is made up from a mass of warriors, maybe thousands strong, well-armed and tightly packed together for good defence. Meanwhile, the "horns" move quickly to the sides and encircle the enemy before attacking, so that they don't know which way to face. The "loins" wait behind the chest to see how the battle's going, and join the fighting when they can have the most effect.

"It's a very strange thing," pondered Mehlokazulu when Sigwelewele had disappeared to encourage his other lieutenants.

"What's so strange, brother?" I asked.

"Well, think about it," he replied. "The white men trade with us. They must know our customs. Yet they've chosen to attack us at harvest time, when food is plentiful, and when so many Zulus are gathering at the King's *kraal* anyway, for the Festival of the First Fruits. If they'd come almost at any other time of the year, recruiting and organizing an army as great as this would have been impossible."

"Perhaps they think we will be easy to defeat?" I said, shivering a little at the thought.

"Maybe they do," he agreed, shaking his head. "But if so, they haven't understood us, and our love for our land."

The *impi* was well armed. Many of the warriors carried rifles along with their stabbing spears and shields. There were men from every regiment. Even old men like the handful of survivors from the *umKhulutshane*, founded long ago by King Dingane, had turned out to help. They were past 70 years old now, their faces lined, their hair grey and receding. Then there were the *uVe*, not much more than twenty years of age, and so younger even than my brothers, keen to show they were as brave as Zulu warriors had ever been.

For the first day or so, the women marched with us and kept the army supplied with food and beer from the royal *kraal*, and from farms we passed on the way. But as we came closer to the border with Natal, we knew the women would be left behind. Then food would be increasingly hard to come by. The cattle would give us a constant supply of milk to drink, but eventually they would have to be slaughtered to provide meals for the warriors. Twenty thousand mouths are a lot to feed!

Although I slept the nights alongside Mehlokazulu, I spent my days a little away from the main *impi*, driving the cattle along with two or three other *udibi*. They were older than me, and at first tended to treat me like a child. I felt lonely and wished I had Sipho with me for company. I missed his mindless chatter and gossip. And despite the fact that we quarrelled sometimes, there's never been anyone better at cheering me up than Sipho. In the end I think he wished he'd stayed with me. As I'd prepared to go to war with Mehlokazulu, he'd set off for kwaSihayo with a face like a rhino.

The *impi* marched slowly for the next two days, and it was no problem to keep pace with it despite the slowness of the cattle.

"Why are we marching so slowly?" I asked Mehlokazulu, as he washed in a stream on the third morning after Ulundi.

"If you're stalking your prey, do you run up to him waving your feathers around?" he answered.

"We could take them by surprise," I said enthusiastically.

"You think so? What about their spies? I suppose they're blind!"

"What spies?" I said surprised.

"Use your common sense! Just as we have men out scouting for signs of the enemy, so does the white man," said Mehlokazulu, rinsing his mouth with water. "We saw horsemen twice yesterday, and once the day before that. They seemed very interested in how many of us there were, and what direction we were headed. You can bet the white men know we're coming. And our scouts tell us the white man's army is stretched out near kwaJimu."

"That's only a day's march from home," I said. There was a mission station at kwaJimu, which Father Simons visited from time to time. The English name for the place was "Rorke's Drift" after a white farmer who'd lived there.

"March slowly, and stay strong," were Mehlokazulu's last brief words on the subject.

After the other *udibi* heard that I'd been there when Kaqwelebana had met her downfall, they began to take a new interest in me. Though they tried to hide it, I knew they were secretly impressed.

"I heard that worms immediately crawled out of her body where she fell," said Tholi, the oldest boy and the unofficial leader. "Is that right?"

I scoffed. "Nobody but Mehlokazulu would know that, and he's never said anything to me," I said. "But he did mention that he killed a cobra very close to the place that same morning. Maybe it was Kaqwelebana coming back to get him!"

"*Ay-ih*," they exclaimed, their eyes opening a little wider at this first-hand information.

The next day the *impi* split into two long parallel columns, and the *inGobamakhosi* spent the night in a hollow to the north side of the hill called Isipezi.

That evening there was a great council, an *indaba*. The commanders were discussing their next moves. Mehlokazulu went to take part and came back chuckling.

"Old man Tshingwayo's having a job holding things together," he said.

I was shocked to hear my brother talk this way. "Didn't everyone hear the King say they should listen to Tshingwayo as if it were he himself?"

"Yes, but the King isn't here, is he?" spluttered Mehlokazulu. "And there are people like Dabulamanzi who think they could do a better job than some old greybeard any day."

There'd been a difference of opinion between those on Dabulamanzi's side who wanted to move straight to the attack, and those with Sigwelewele who thought the warriors would be fresher after a night's rest. Besides, they said, to attack on the day before the new moon would bring bad luck. After hours of argument, the vote was to hold back. So by high sun the next morning, the whole Zulu *impi* had marched up on to the Nqutu plateau, with the *udibi* and our cattle trotting behind. This high, rocky plain ran gently down towards

74

the hill named Isandlwana. I'd heard of this place. It was famous because of its shape – like a lion sitting on its haunches. In the middle of the Nqutu plateau was a deep ravine, a third of a day's march in length. I watched from a distance, at my station beside the cattle, as the Zulu *impi* descended into it in their thousands, climbing down over the boulders to huddle quietly in its depths by the stream that flowed along its floor.

It was a remarkable thing. You could be a stone's throw from the edge of the ravine and be completely unaware that a whole army was camped below. If the British white men had heard a Zulu army was on its way to fight them, now they'd be wondering where it had gone.

Late in the afternoon, I wandered around on the plateau with the other *udibi* checking that the cattle were all right. If any white men saw us, they'd think nothing of it. Just a few poor Zulu children tending their miserable cows!

The cattle had found one of the very few patches of poor pasture on the plateau about a mile or so from the *impi*, and were grazing peacefully. It was a beautiful evening. The late sun was warm on my back, and the land and sky formed strips of gold grey and blue which blurred into one another as the light slowly started to fade. It was a sight that made me want to skip for joy one moment, and sad the next. To think death could take this beauty away from you, suddenly and without warning! I left the others and skirted the plain, until the ground fell away and I could see the foot of Isandlwana before me, where I could imagine the lion's front paws to be.

There, in the shadow of the hill, lay the white man's camp. A long line of tents and wagons sprawled out right across the gently sloping ground. For the first time I understood what we faced. From what I saw, I guessed that the British army must be almost as large in number as ours. But what also struck me was the difference between the two sides. Our warriors were hunched up in the ravine, keeping silent, bracing themselves to fight to the death. The white men were all over the place. Some seemed to be playing games, throwing a ball to each other. Others were sitting in chairs outside their tents, sunning themselves. They looked completely unprepared for the battle to come, and I ran back to the ravine to tell my brother it was so.

When at last I found Mehlokazulu among the mass of silent men, he was talking with Sigwelewele. They listened gravely.

"The white men haven't bothered to defend

themselves," I said enthusiastically. "Their wagons are in a great long line. We could easily attack them. Surely they ought to have formed them into a circle, if they wanted to be safe?"

Sigwelewele's laugh came from his belly, and it made his chest shake. "So Jabulani's making his play to be commander of the *impi*, Mehlokazulu? Eh?"

I thought he was making fun of me, and I felt my cheeks growing hot. He saw my embarrassment, and changed his tone.

"No, no, listen! You're quite right, Jabulani. It's very peculiar. And what you say confirms what other scouts have been telling me. But if a Zulu *udibi* can understand this, why are the red soldiers so blind? That's the question."

Other scouts! I grew two inches taller at the thought that I was included with the *other* scouts! "So, will we attack tomorrow?" I asked.

Mehlokazulu shook his head. "It's a bad day, Jabulani. There's a new moon. It's safest to wait." He turned to his commander. "Sigwelewele, since the white men are so casual, shouldn't we still send messengers to see if we can make peace? Isn't it worth one last try?"

"Perhaps," was all that Sigwelewele would say.

The next day dawned chilly and clear. I was glad to

have the excuse to rise early from where I slept hunched up in a hollow on the ravine's edge, tend the cattle, and maybe then take fresh milk to Mehlokazulu and the men around him. They'd settled in for a few days on short rations until the battle had been fought, and on this cold morning, they'd be desperate for anything to eat or drink.

With the other *udibi* I climbed up on to the plateau and crossed to where the cattle squatted. We'd just finished our milking when from the corner of my eye I saw the dust kicking up from horses' hooves a mile or so away. A band of riders at least a dozen strong was hustling towards us, and I glimpsed flashes of red about the chests of the men. I called to the others.

We acted thoughtlessly. We ran for our lives, leaving the cattle to fend for themselves, scattering milk from our calabashes as we went. We reached the lip of the ravine and scattered down its ledges and scree slopes before the horsemen arrived. It was too late, of course. We'd been too quick on our feet for them to capture us, but they'd seen where we'd gone. Standing at the top of the ravine, his horse pecking and rearing underneath him, a single British soldier fired a shot into the air to signal our position.

In that moment, what Tshingwayo or Sigwelewele

thought no longer mattered. New moon rising or not, the hotheads of the *umCijo* regiment, nearest to the British horsemen, jumped to their feet and swarmed up the ravine in pursuit of the red soldiers. Not wishing to be outdone, the other regiments followed them at a run.

As the warriors continued to pour up towards the lip of the ravine, stretching and pulsing like a swarm of bees, I found my place at Mehlokazulu's side. I was distraught that I'd helped give away our position to the invading army. How I wished I'd shown a bit more presence of mind. If we'd stayed with the cattle, the British patrol might just have ridden on by.

"I'm sorry," I said half-walking, half-running at his shoulder. "I'm so sorry."

"What for, little brother?" he said. "You did what you thought was right. It may be for the best, after all. We shall see."

Out on the plateau, there was chaos and confusion. As the *impi* burst into the open everyone was shouting and pointing, expecting to fight at any moment. But gradually, as they realized there was no immediate danger, an organized army began to emerge. The various regiments shuffled into their stations in the left and right horns, the chest and the loins. They traded insults as they passed each other, goading their rivals with taunts.

"Don't worry, old men," the *inGobamakhosi* shouted at the *umKhulutshane*. "We'll look after you if the going gets tough."

"How are you coping without your wet-nurses, lads?" came the reply.

For the first time in my life, as the *impi* prepared to drive down towards the British line, the fear inside me rolled forward into complete panic. It wasn't death itself which now terrified me so much as how I might die. I imagined the slow, griping agony of a cruelly twisted knife.

I saw Mehlokazulu reach into the pouch at his waist and take a pinch of snuff. He sneezed loudly, and shook his head vigorously, wincing at the effect.

"For the fighting spirit," he smiled. "Want some?"

I shook my head. At that moment Mehlokazulu seemed to me to be incredibly calm – and incredibly brave.

"What can I do, Mehlokazulu?" I said in a voice that sounded unlike my own, dry and squeaky.

"Do as you've been doing," he said patiently. "Join the other *udibi* and make sure you stay with our cattle," he said. "Only, drive them down parallel to the left horn, but inside and behind it. Use the cattle as cover for yourselves, and wait for word."

I wanted to reach out and embrace my brother, but there was no time even to clasp hands. I couldn't bear the thought that I might never see him alive again. As Mehlokazulu had instructed, we held the cattle back, and I settled, with my own thoughts, on a rock which jutted up from the plain. I whispered a prayer to the ancestors for Mehlokazulu's safety.

The chest of the *impi* marched on towards the British camp. The horns split and veered to the left and right, eerily silent as they made their way across the dusty ground.

I watched closely as the left horn, including the *inGobamakhosi*, slowly picked its way along. Then from the distance I saw grey and white puffs of smoke from the British rifles, heard their sound, and saw the *inGobamakhosi* drop to the ground and take cover as the British bullets struck into the men at the front of the column.

I clambered over some boulders to get a better view. A few lines of smoke drifted high into the still sky above the dark grey line of the British camp. Although the right horn of the Zulu army had disappeared from view now, snaking far around the plateau to outflank the British, I could see the chest sinking lower in the plain towards the camp. Facing it was a line of red soldiers, already many spear lengths from their camp. The white men had left the safety and cover of their wagons and advanced into the open.

The left horn was pinned down by the British fire. It had stopped moving. Soon so did the chest. I could see and hear the fierce volleys of shots fired by both sides, and though many of our warriors were lying on the rocky ground, it was difficult to say whether they were taking cover or whether they were wounded.

Actually, that isn't true. In my heart of hearts I knew that a great number of the bodies strewn at the front of the chest under the growing canopy of smoke must be dead. At the time I shut the thought from my mind.

A whistle came from below me. It was Tholi, the most senior of the *udibi*. He waved his arms frantically, and I scrambled over the rocks to be at his side.

"They've sent word," he said. "We've got to drive the cattle down closer towards the rear of the left horn. Come on! Stir yourself!"

We prodded the beasts into action, thumping their flanks with our sticks and driving them down the plain until we were on the heels of the older warriors at the rear of the left horn. The firing grew louder as we approached and every blast hurt our ears. But even as we moved forward I thought I noticed that the guns appeared to fire less often.

I asked a toothless old man, an *umKhulutshane*, how the battle was going. He smiled a grim and knowing smile.

"The white man has fired his gun very often," he said. "He can't fire it for ever. Maybe he's running out of bullets!"

The *inGobamakhosi* took over the cattle, pushing them through to the front of the line, then beating and kicking them on down towards the red soldiers.

As I stood and watched, the cattle thundered into the enemy, causing panic as they searched for help and ammunition. In behind the cattle came the *inGobamakhosi*, glad to get in close now and put their stabbing spears to work. The white men reeled backwards, trying first to avoid the cattle's flying hooves and then our warriors' fierce attack.

The red soldiers who didn't fall began to run, and soon there was a full-scale retreat, with our left horn charging on with menacing shouts down towards the line of wagons in their main camp, closer and ever closer. I followed at a safe distance, with Tholi and the others.

To our right we saw the men of the chest, who'd

been pinned down by the British fire, summon their courage, and rise from their knees. They also began to push forward with a mighty roar towards the British lines, inspired by the royal battle-cry of "*uSuthu*". This time it was sheer force of numbers which caused the red soldiers to give way, overwhelmed by the black river of warriors which surged across them.

Then the *umCijo*, leading the Zulu right horn, thrust a spear deep into the British heart. I saw them rush in behind the defenders of the British camp. The red soldiers there looked in panic first one way and then the other. There were Zulus on three sides of them now. They couldn't decide whether to stand up to the chest or turn to try and deal with the horns who'd come in at their flanks.

The battle was over in a few minutes more. There was terrible slaughter. I saw soldiers slit open from neck to abdomen, limbs hacked off, dreadful things done by men to other men. I watched as one red soldier, surrounded by a crowd of our men, turned a pistol on himself. Where the British had no more bullets they used their bare hands, grappling desperately with our warriors to stave off the attack. In the shadow of the sphinx of Isandlwana, the red soldiers fought like lions themselves.

Then something happened to make us all tremble. The sun went dark, even though it was mid-afternoon. It seemed as if the world might end then and there. Was it an omen for good or evil?

"What's happening," I said to Tholi, my voice shaking.

His eyes were very wide and white in the eerie half-light. "I don't know," he said. "I don't know!"

When the light returned, I ran and found Mehlokazulu. His face and body were smeared with blood, and he was exhausted by the fighting, but he was triumphant.

"Victory," he shouted, not to me so much as to the whole battlefield, "*uSuthu*! Victory and freedom!"

Behind him, I could see Zulus tearing the clothing from the bodies of white men, taking trophies wherever they could find them, from the pockets of the dead men, from their tents and wagons. They were pulling out medals, knives, and cooking utensils. They were drinking from the bottles they'd found. Some were mutilating the bodies of the white men, taking the power from them as they cut out their hearts and livers. They slaughtered even the dogs and horses the white men had brought with them. I was learning the truth about war, and about the madness that comes into warriors' hearts. I found myself turning away to be sick.

A warrior who stood near us gave a low laugh when he saw me, pale-faced and sitting on my haunches, struggling for air. He said cruelly, "Does this cur belong to you, Mehlokazulu? I thought everyone in your family was used to blood-letting. I'm surprised you haven't trained him better."

In other circumstances Mehlokazulu might have responded violently to such an insult. But with the battle still raging in his eyes he said harshly to me, "Pull yourself together, Jabulani! Act as if you're worthy of your father's name, or go home!"

I was deeply wounded. I thought what had been said was unfair, but then again, I wished I'd not allowed my feelings to show. Maybe such things shouldn't come between brothers, but my admiration for Mehlokazulu was scarred at that moment. I thought he should have spoken up for me.

After the battle at Isandlwana, the white men fled. Our warriors hadn't eaten for more than a day and a half, and there were hundreds of wounded men who needed carrying to safety. With the other *udibi*, Tholi and I did what we could to help.

"There's another over here," we called, when we found a man who might still live. "But don't bother with that one. He's gone."

86

After the battle, those warriors who were still able-bodied picked up their wounded comrades and carried them on their backs, sometimes for miles. Between us all, we saved many lives.

Others were beyond saving, and begged for the swift thrust of a knife under the left armpit to carry them out of their agony.

Some of the commanders still wanted to set off in chase of the British, even if that meant disobeying the King's orders and crossing the border. Mehlokazulu would have none of it, and was prepared to argue with his commander. Sigwelewele had rushed up to him, anxious to gather the *inGobamakhosi* together for more glory.

"Dabulamanzi and the *iNdluyengwe* are already on the road in the footsteps of the white men," he blustered. "Do you want him to steal all the credit? The *umCijo* are already crowing that they beat the red soldiers on their own!"

"Forget the empty heads of the *umCijo*, Sigwelewele! And remember that Dabulamanzi is a fool and a self-seeker," replied Mehlokazulu, calmer and more himself now. "He was never happy that old man Tshingwayo was made commander-in-chief. Now he sees a chance to claim the victory was all his doing. Let him go, and spare our men! Look at them,

Sigwelewele! They've had enough. The road to Natal's a road too far. A road that shouldn't be taken! Not if you listened to the King properly! Have you forgotten that he explicitly warned us *not* to cross the border?"

To his credit, Sigwelewele heard my brother's words, and allowed Dabulamanzi to plunge on alone to kwaJimu.

As the sun set for the second time that awful, omen-filled day, many men stumbled off to nearby *kraals* to rest and find food. Some, like us, bivouacked with shields and sleeping mats through a short, moonless night when angry purple clouds scudded across the bright stars. The groans of wounded warriors carried far on the wind, and more than once I was woken by piercing screams, like the cries of hunting jackals.

In the morning the warriors dispersed. I followed a silent Mehlokazulu back to kwaSihayo, accompanied by other warriors who lived nearby. The village had been hastily rebuilt with a few flimsy thatched huts, but they were very poorly made. Scorch marks disfigured the turf. Usually the place would have been leaping with life, but now it too was silent, apart from the sound of tears.

For everyone was crying and wailing, men and women alike, despite our success in the battle. So many had died already, and everywhere I looked there were casualties who might yet give in to death. They were pale and bleeding, ghosts of men. No one was working in the fields that day, and the cattle had been left unmilked. A *sangoma* went the rounds, handing out medicine. Everyone was to take it, for healing, and to ward off evil spirits. It tasted awful, and I didn't dare ask what had gone into the foul-smelling brew. When he'd finished ministering to us, the *sangoma* went out and dosed the cattle too, muttering incantations around their puzzled heads.

I saw Sipho in the distance, and we waved a shy and solemn greeting at each other. This wasn't a day for games or gossip, and I think we both felt awkward, having gone our separate ways the previous week.

A day later even greater numbers of wounded men began to arrive at the village, stumbling and staring of eye. They were *iNdluyengwe*, Dabulamanzi's men, who'd defied the King and pursued the British to kwaJimu. They staggered in on damaged legs, holding on to each other for support, trying to staunch the flow from weeping gashes in their mutilated bodies. Rumours began to circulate about what might have happened.

Sipho sidled by our hut, and this time I grabbed the chance to talk with him.

"It's good to see you again, my friend," I said. "Do you know what happened down there?"

"I've heard it all went wrong for Dabulamanzi," said Sipho in hushed tones. "I talked to one of the warriors who came in from kwaJimu today. The white men had fortified the mission station. They weren't great in number, but they had powerful guns and much ammunition. Our warriors couldn't get near them. They're saying hundreds of Zulus were killed in a few hours."

"Why did we continue attacking if it was so hopeless?" I asked.

Sipho came closer. "Apparently, when they gathered for the assault on kwaJimu, the first thing which met their eyes was a Zulu swaying in the wind. He was hanging upside down from a meat-hook attached to a tree. His body had been so badly beaten it was almost unrecognizable. The white men had tortured him before they'd killed him. Our warriors needed little encouragement to fight to the death after that."

Sometimes my friend's stories were so fantastic I didn't know whether to believe him. But after what I'd seen at Isandlwana, I didn't doubt him for a moment. Men can become like animals in war.

Over the next few weeks, life very slowly went back to normal in kwaSihayo. The fences and huts began to be restored. The women returned to the fields. But tempers were easily frayed in those days. I saw several fights between exhausted and drunk warriors, and learned that mourning takes people many different ways.

One evening I saw Mehlokazulu gathering himself for a journey. I was surprised. I'd become used to being at his side, even though things between us had been strained since the incident on the battlefield at Isandlwana. The thought hadn't crossed my mind that he might go off without me.

"What's going on, brother?" I said as innocently as I could.

He had the grace to look sheepish. "I'm going to Ulundi," he said.

"Why's that?" I asked.

He looked at me as if I was stupid. "You think it's all over now, Jabulani? Do you imagine we can just let

91

sleeping dogs lie? Accept the loss of all those warriors unavenged? As if the white men won't return anyway. Grow up!" And he turned his back on me, and continued to tie up his bundle. His fingers were clumsy that day. I'd have tied it far more expertly.

I felt ashamed that he obviously no longer thought me worthy to be his *udibi*. I gave it one last try. In a small voice I said, "Am I coming with you?"

He straightened, and looked at me in a way that suggested I was very tiresome. For a moment I thought he was just going to brush me off. But then something made him change his mind, and he spoke to me more gently.

"This time let me go alone. It'll all be soldier's talk. You're more use here, helping make kwaSihayo fit for your father's return."

There was a long pause. I stood there, waiting, watching him fumble with his belongings. Finally he gave in. "Listen! If I haven't come back in three weeks, make your way to Ulundi, and find me there. All right?"

I thought to myself, *You wait, Mehlokazulu. I'll show you. Just give me a chance, and I'll prove myself as much a warrior as any Zulu!*

After three dull and frustrating weeks there was no sign of Mehlokazulu, so I took him at his word. I said my goodbyes to kwaSihayo, and picked my way across the hills towards Ulundi. This time I knew where I was going. I was sorry to leave Sipho behind, but perhaps not as sorry as he was to be left. We clasped hands and promised we would always be friends. To be truthful, apart from him there wasn't much else I was going to miss. After the excitement of Isandlwana, and a glimpse of the bigger world, life in kwaSihayo had come to seem very slow and sleepy.

When I reached Ulundi I found an even larger city of huts sprawled across the plain than before. If the Zulu *impi* had lost thousands of men at Isandlwana and kwaJimu (I heard some say 5,000) then many thousands more had joined the cause. I met Zulus from the coast, who'd always had the reputation for being cowards. I met Zulus from the northwest, who hadn't always been King Cetshwayo's most loyal subjects. I even heard Zulu women breathing revenge against the red soldiers, saying that if their menfolk had no stomach for battle, well then they'd do the job themselves.

"What we need," thundered Sigwelewele, "is one great battle." We were sitting outside his hut –

Mehlokazulu, the other junior officers of the *inGobamakhosi*, and their *udibi*, including me.

"One in which we get to settle the scores, and not the *umCijo*," said the newly promoted Shenkwana, trying to score points. There was a mutter of agreement. It still hurt the *inGobamakhosi* that the *umCijo* were so overbearing about their supposed brilliance at Isandlwana. Even in a day or so at Ulundi, I'd noticed that the *umCijo* seized every chance of a joke against the *inGobamakhosi*'s supposed slowness of foot or lack of manhood.

"Is that the King's opinion then – about a single battle?" asked Mehlokazulu quietly. My brother always seemed to be the one holding back the rashness of his superior officer.

"Well yes, as a matter of fact I think it is!" answered Sigwelewele defensively. "Though of course he's put Dabulamanzi in his place after kwaJimu. There'll be no repeat of such stupidity."

"He should have paid for it with his life," said Shenkwana.

Everyone looked at him disapprovingly.

"Dabulamanzi has the coastal people in the palm of his hand," said Mehlokazulu firmly. "And we need their help. The King may not like it, but he has to be

94

careful with that man. As you should be with your tongue, Shenkwana."

I stifled a giggle. I'd never liked Shenkwana very much.

Of course, someone was always going to suffer for the losses at kwaJimu. In the end it had been Tshingwayo who'd caught the King's wrath. It was said he should have controlled Dabulamanzi better. He'd been replaced by the slightly younger Mnyamana, who was King Cetshwayo's highly trusted chief minister.

"And now we have Mnyamana to tell us what to do," muttered Sigwelewele. "The fellow who the King sent to find a peace with the British, and who failed even in that. The man's no fighter. At least Tshingwayo knew one end of a spear from the other."

"King Cetshwayo would have done far better appointing you," said Shenkwana, trying to regain his leader's favour. Sigwelewele shot him a look of contempt.

"Well, how can I disagree with the opinion of such a great military mind?" he said. Several of those who sat around, Mehlokazulu included, hooted with laughter.

At Eshowe, a day's march away from Ulundi near the coast, lay a fort. It was under siege by a large band of our warriors and was being stoutly defended by red soldiers. The siege had already lasted for more than a week.

"They can't get out," Mehlokazulu said to me a couple of days after the conversation with Sigwelewele. "But we can't get in. Their rifles are too powerful."

"So it's a stalemate?" I said.

"It may not stay that way," replied Mehlokazulu. "We have spies inside the British lines way to the south, and they say a great British army is about to march on Eshowe. Their commander-in-chief, a man called Lord Chelmsford, is organizing things himself. He's determined to break the siege. Apparently he's a very warlike man."

"And will we stand and fight?"

"You heard Sigwelewele," Mehlokazulu said with a grim smile. "There are many who think like him, and feel we can destroy the British army. Prepare yourself, Jabulani! Tomorrow we go on the road. It's certain Sigwelewele will get his 'great battle' sooner or later!"

How many men marched and ran towards Eshowe I don't know. They were beyond counting. The dust we raised was enough to blacken the sun. The might of the Zulu nation traipsed backwards and forwards past the fort shouting to the red soldiers to come out and fight.

"Come on, Johnnie," the warriors shouted. "Where are you? Are you afraid of poor, simple black men?"

No answer came, not even a single shot. They weren't stupid. They knew they were outnumbered.

On past Eshowe we went in very high spirits, singing our way to the south, spoiling for a fight – a fight which never came. Two days we waited for the British army to show, but then came a message from our spies to say there'd been a delay to the British plans. Lord Chelmsford had decided his army wasn't ready enough: the fort at Eshowe would have to look after itself. Mnyamana deliberated with the regiments about whether to attack anyway, and decided against it.

"He's right, of course," cursed Mehlokazulu. "The prize isn't worth the losses we'd take."

But like many of the warriors Mehlokazulu was fidgeting with frustration. He couldn't keep still. For three days he'd been keyed up, sensing that there'd never be a better chance to settle things once and for all in our favour. Perhaps he missed Nkubikazulu too.

"If I saw a red soldier," he growled, pacing up and down, hands gripped tightly together, "any red soldier,

I'd kill him very slowly with my fingers around his neck. Quick death from an *iklwa*'s too good for any of them."

The rest of the men were quarrelsome and edgy too. If the King let them wait any longer, the anger inside them might spill over against each other instead of the enemy.

A few days later we were on the move again, this time to the northwest.

"First Eshowe, now Khambula! Why can't the King make up his mind?" I heard Mehlokazulu ask Sigwelewele as the regiment pounded along.

His commander shrugged. "What does a wounded leopard do when the hunters attack him from two sides?" he said. "He's still dangerous, Mehlokazulu, but just more unpredictable."

I'd already learned from Mehlokazulu that not only were the white men planning to attack from the south, they had a garrison at Khambula in the northwest too. Word had come in that from there they'd begun to attack the Qulusi Zulus in their *kraals* at nearby Hlobane.

Lindelani, the *udibi* who attended Sigwelewele, had been born at Hlobane. He was senior to me, a tall boy I liked very much. He commanded great respect.

Sigwelewele turned to him. "You know Hlobane, don't you, Lindelani?"

Lindelani nodded.

"Then take Jabulani with you. Be my eyes at Hlobane. Start at dawn, and tell me what you see. I want to know how many red soldiers there are and how well armed. We need to decide how to spread our forces. Go and earn your keep, Lindelani."

Maybe Sigwelewele spoke sternly, but I could see that Lindelani was precious to him.

As I'd have been among the paths around kwaSihayo, so was Lindelani that day on the trails leading up into green Hlobane. Every rock, every blade of grass seemed to have a story attached to it. He loved his home ground as if it was a part of himself. Now this way, now that, we tiptoed stealthily over the hills.

I'm usually a very happy person. Generally speaking, however bad one day is I still wake up smiling the next. Everyone's always said so. So where did the evil spirit come from that troubled me that day? From the moment my eyes opened that morning,

I'd felt a premonition, a rumbling tremor in my stomach and hands.

I can only tell you that when we turned a corner and found ourselves staring into the faces of the British soldiers it came as no surprise.

Lindelani let out an involuntary "*Ay-ih*!" and then, as if any encouragement was needed, shouted at me, "Run!"

We turned and fled. There were ten red soldiers with one man on horseback at their rear. The two of us zigzagged across a piece of rising ground, stretching desperately to reach cover, but the lie of the land allowed our pursuers a clear shot. I took a glance over my shoulder, saw a soldier drop to his knees to steady his aim, heard Lindelani shout a warning, and then a second or so later my stomach curdled at the sound of his scream as a bullet sliced into his leg. For an instant I stopped in my tracks, unsure whether to stay or go.

Even in his agony, Lindelani yelled, "Go, go, Jabulani! Save yourself!" A bullet whistled past my ears. I swear I felt its trail of wind. More shots rang out, echoing off the rocks, and I thought I heard Lindelani cry out one last time.

Part of me wanted to stay and tend his last moments, but I knew it would have been the end of me too and my feet kept flying forwards. The only small comfort I could take was that Lindelani would have preferred to die nowhere else than in his beloved Hlobane.

Miraculously, weaving a course through the maze of thorns and rubble, at the limits of my strength, I somehow escaped death or capture and made it back to the *impi* and Sigwelewele's side.

When he saw me approaching him, by myself and in distress, Sigwelewele's brow furrowed.

"We were taken by surprise," I stammered, suddenly aware of how my hands shook, how weak my legs felt.

"And Lindelani?" muttered Sigwelewele, so quietly I could scarcely hear him.

I swallowed. "Dead. At least, I think so."

Sigwelewele showed no reaction, not a blink, not a crease in the face. "The soldiers. How many are there? How are they disposed?"

I swallowed again. My head swam. I couldn't think what to say. There was nothing helpful I could say.

"I don't know. We never got close enough to see their army. We only saw the red soldiers who chased us... Ten, maybe?"

Sigwelewele said nothing. He just turned away, and stood staring into the far distance, wordless, expressionless. I knew I'd failed him, and it seemed he wanted nothing more to do with me. For a second time, when it mattered, I felt I'd let myself down. Why couldn't I ever do the right thing? What could I do to prove I was worthy of my father? There had to be something.

Who took the decision, and who provided the information which Lindelani and I had failed to bring back, I don't know, but the next day the whole Zulu *impi* of perhaps 15,000 men began to move faster and faster towards the garrison at Khambula, sweeping south of Hlobane. As we passed by we saw occasional British scouts on the crest of the hills hundreds of feet above watching us curiously. The *impi* must have been an awesome sight as it ran along the valley floor, a river of feathers and animal skin, a venomous snake of an army, driving on to strike at the British defences. The horns divided with the *inGobamakhosi* this time to the right and at the front of the movement. Sigwelewele drove us on relentlessly and angrily. It seemed to me he was channelling his fury at Lindelani's death into the honour of the regiment. I trailed miserably along in Mehlokazulu's wake. No one spoke to me, although probably only because they were concentrating on their own thoughts. That day I found it very hard to keep up with the pace of the advance.

As we neared the British lines, picking our way between the thorn bushes, the *inGobamakhosi* warriors began to make a hissing sound. "*Zhi, ZHI,*" they went. "*Zhi, ZHI.*" With every moment the noise grew louder, a sound designed to frighten, to cause panic. It echoed from the rocks all around us and made our great numbers seem even larger than they were. Determination was written on every face in the regiment. This time they'd take second place to no one. They'd be first at the enemy if they possibly could, first into his tents, first to strip him of his power, before the boastful *umCijo* or the taunting *uThulwana*.

Only Mehlokazulu had his doubts. "We're too far ahead," he muttered to me. "What's got into Sigwelewele? Has he lost his senses? If he's not careful we'll be there long before the left horn. What's the good of glory, if we lose the whole battle as a result?"

Mehlokazulu tried to slow the men in his companies down, shouting over their heads that they were putting the whole operation in danger, but the warriors were carried along by the rhythm of the advance, and Mehlokazulu couldn't get far enough forward to hold them back. They crashed on and on towards the British lines, and I found myself carried with them, on a second wind of strength and courage.

From far ahead I heard the enemy open up with their guns. Volley on volley of shots began to echo louder and louder, threatening to burst my ears apart. Violent explosions began to make the ground shake. Smoke drifted in among us, cutting us off from each other. Suddenly I realized I'd lost sight of Mehlokazulu. I found that I was stepping over bodies of the dead and wounded, started to see men cut down by cannon and rifle fire on either side of me, and by instinct threw myself to the ground with them. I was astonished to see that grovelling on their bellies around me were Zulu warriors who were still very much alive. They were firing their rifles randomly and gibbering nonsense. They seemed to have lost the will to move forward under the hail of bullets and shells directed towards us. I felt a mad surge of energy run through me. It lifted and thrilled me. I saw a chance for glory, to make everything all right.

"What do you think you're doing?" I shouted to anyone and no one. "Don't you see? You'll all be killed if you stay here. Get up, you cowards, and move on. Call yourself warriors? Think of your honour! Think of your ancestors!"

Unarmed though I was, I stood up and hurled myself into whatever lay out beyond the smoke.

I ran and ran, screaming the worst curses I knew, hurtling completely alone into the enemy lines. There was thunder in my ears, but no lightning struck me down as I threw myself at the red soldiers, lashing out at their faces with my fists. They must have been amazed to see a Zulu boy suddenly dive into their shallow trenches, but in a moment they'd swarmed over me and pinned me to the ground, still kicking and swearing. For the next hour, while the battle raged around me, I lay struggling under the body of an English soldier as he handed up ammunition to his comrades, muttering to himself.

The British took very few prisoners in the battle at Khambula. No more than fifteen or so of us were kept behind a stockade at their camp in the days that followed. The reason for this was very simple – the numbers of Zulu dead were enormous. From where the soldiers held us captive, I could look down on to the fields in front of Khambula, where the birds of prey had gathered to pick at the bones of the warriors' bodies. In those first days, under the warm sun, the stench became suffocating.

"It is a terrible thing," said an *umCijo* warrior who peered mournfully through the fence at the field of corpses in front of us. "*Ay-ih!* We Zulus must learn to shoot straight."

"The *inGobamakhosi* shoot straight enough," I said, trying to keep up both our spirits, hoping against hope that Mehlokazulu and Sigwelewele were safe.

"Listen, boy," he said roughly, "there's your evidence. How many wounded red soldiers do you see? And how many dead Zulus? *inGobamakhosi* as well as *umCijo!*"

Our rifles had been no match for the British weapons. We'd been shooting from higher ground and our bullets had gone over their heads. Their mechanical guns, cannon and rifles had torn into our lines. Waves of Zulus had risen towards the incoming fire, and been cut down. I was miserable that I had been captured, but in my heart I knew I had been very lucky indeed.

Eventually all fifteen of us were paraded in front of the British chief, whose name was Wood, a short man with a very red face. He himself could only stutter the occasional word of Zulu, but with him was another taller white man who spoke our language very well. Wood talked to us through him. He wanted to know all about the different regiments, how they dressed and what had made them famous. He explained that the British had regiments in their army too. They also had their rivalries, and individual uniforms, just like us. A few Zulu tongues began to loosen. Wood listened intently to them as they began to boast about their exploits in war, hunched forward on his chair, resting his chin on his hands. Suddenly he changed to a different tack.

"After we fought you at Isandlwana," he said quietly, stroking the hair which grew on his upper lip, "we treated some of your wounded countrymen, and made them better." He stood up and began to pace backwards and forwards. "Do you know what happened?"

No one replied, but I could guess the answer. I expect we all could.

"No?" he continued. "Well I'll tell you. As soon as our backs were turned, to repay us for our mercy, these men attacked us in our own camp."

There was a muttering among the prisoners, as if to say, "*Of course! What else did you expect?*"

"Very well," he continued. "But now that we hold all of you here behind bars, can you tell me why I shouldn't just give orders to shoot the lot of you straight away? Eh?"

There was a silence. The other warriors looked at each other, but no one could find a suitable reply. A fear began inside me that if somebody didn't say something quickly, Wood might carry out his threat. Taking a step forward I said, in the best English I could remember, "There's an excellent reason why you shouldn't kill us, *nkosi*. You may have heard that it's the custom of Zulus to take no prisoners. But a white man called Father Simons once told me your customs were different, and better. He also told me that I should forgive my enemies over and over again."

For a moment the pinkness left the man Wood's face, and he became more truly white than he'd been before. In that instant I wondered if we might all pay for my boldness. But then he began to chuckle. His laughter rumbled up from deep in his stomach and trickled out at the top of his head. Through his translator, he told the other Zulus what I'd said and then added, "Watch this boy! He may end up as your King one day. And he's quite right. Forgiveness is a great thing."

My cheekiness worked. After a few more questions, Wood dismissed all fifteen of us without delay, promising safe passage out of the British camp. He thanked the warriors for their interesting information, and wished us happy lives.

But as we stood to leave, the *umCijo* warrior I'd spoken to earlier came up to me and clasped hands. He gripped me to him closely and whispered viciously in my ear, "Better you had never been born, boy, than to say such traitorous things to the enemy. I would never forgive these men anything, and I don't expect them to forgive me. When we are outside the camp, I will show you what an *umCijo* thinks of treachery."

His voice was bitter and terrifying, and in that instant I knew my life was in danger at his hands. I started to stammer an explanation, but at that moment Wood came towards us. The *umCijo* cast him a look of disdain, and slunk away slowly out of the camp, with a meaningful backwards glance at me. As I stood there, nervous and shaking, Wood asked me who I was and where I came from.

I told him.

"And how did you learn your English?"

"From that same Father Simons," I said, "at the mission station near kwaSihayo."

I assumed that since they were both white men he'd know Father Simons, but I could see from his face it wasn't so. He went on to ask me about my real father, and life in the *kraal*. At last he said, with kindness in his voice, "Well, I should think you'd want to go back to your people now, wouldn't you Jabulani? Hurry now, or the others will be far away down the road ahead of you."

I thought of what the *umCijo* warrior had said and stayed where I was, hopping from foot to foot.

"Go on," he repeated. "Be off with you now!"

Still I hung back, fidgeting.

"If it's all right with you, *nkosi*," I said, "perhaps I could stay for a while?"

Puzzled, he paused and looked at me hard. "How would I know you weren't a spy?" he said challengingly.

I had no answer for that. He was right. There was no way he could know.

"Exactly," he continued. "So, go home, Jabulani. You want to see your father again, don't you? And be with your brothers?" He spoke more quietly. "I have sons, far away back in England. I know how much I should like to see them!"

A wind was blowing in my head. My thoughts were being spun round and round. Aside from the *umCijo*'s words, at that moment I felt that if I went home, I'd be returning to disgrace. At Isandlwana, without meaning to, I'd betrayed our position. Then, when I'd been faced with the reality of death on the battlefield I'd shown a lack of spirit. I'd lost Sigwelewele's confidence at Hlobane. Finally I'd lost my head in the heat of battle at Khambula, and been captured. Who would want to know me now? I wasn't even sure Mehlokazulu was still alive. I grasped at the one last root that might save me falling down the cliff.

"I'll be your *udibi*," I said. "I'm very good, *nkosi*. I promise I'll look after you very well. You'll see!"

And with that, Colonel Wood's rumbling laugh began a second time. "All right, Jabulani," he said. "You've convinced me. A Zulu boy who speaks English may be of use when it comes to peace-making, after all. Particularly one who has such a way with words!"

April – June 1879

In a few days the British army and I packed up camp, and moved south west across the border out of Zulu country and towards safety. It would only be for a while, the soldiers agreed. In a month or two they'd be back to finish things off, when reinforcements had arrived from England.

As the straggle of wagons pitched and bumped its way along, I wondered why the red soldiers still seemed so careless about guarding their lines, even after what had happened at Isandlwana. On either side of the path the grass rose high. If there'd been 1,000 Zulus lying in wait they'd never have been seen. Why hadn't we concentrated on ambushing the red soldiers as they moved, rather than fighting the battles in a way that suited them?

And it took the British army so long to get anywhere too. A journey the Zulu *impi* could easily manage in a day seemed to take the British a week. Each stream we came to was a major obstacle, the horses and oxen straining and stumbling down one sandy bank and then up the other.

A huge herd of cattle trailed along beside the British army. I earned my keep by helping to look after them, under the eye of grey-haired, stiff-legged Corporal Harrison, the quartermaster's deputy. The cattle understood me as well as the ones at kwaSihayo, which wasn't any great surprise. Some of them probably were the cattle from kwaSihayo.

As I walked alongside them I realized we could have driven the cattle off, and starved the British to defeat as well. But we hadn't understood how short of food the white man was. Perhaps we'd assumed just because he was white he was rich and had everything he needed. I was shocked to find just how wrong we'd been.

In fact the British soldiers were desperately hungry, not just like Zulus on the battle path for a few days at a time, but *all* the time. They didn't know how to live off the land, which plants could help you stay fit and alert when there was no other food to be had, where to find water at times of shortage. I found myself showing the soldiers which roots to eat, and which to avoid. At first they didn't trust me – they thought I might be trying to poison them – but over a few days they learned that I was right, and knew much more about such things than they did.

I'd always called them the "red soldiers" because of

the colour of their clothing, but up close there wasn't much that was red left about them. What they wore hung from them in shreds, torn to pieces by the bush.

They smelled so much that I used to avoid getting too close. We Zulus are always washing, it's true. But though I saw the red soldiers drink water greedily, they rarely seemed to use it for bathing.

They drank other things too, whenever they got the chance. Once we finally crossed the border, the soldiers built themselves a proper camp on flat rocky ground which had a view to all sides. The third morning we were there, after the first meal of the day, I heard the rattle of their drums and the blowing of horns. I asked Corporal Harrison what was going on.

"You watch this," he said with a grimace, "and take it as a lesson, young Jabulani."

A soldier was pushed into the middle of the camp where there was empty ground, and made to kneel down. The shirt was ripped from his back. It was obvious he was going to be beaten.

"What has he done?" I asked the Corporal.

"He stole from the stores, didn't he?" said Harrison. "Worse than that he stole liquor, and got himself drunk on it. And even worse, it was the Colonel's best malt he nicked."

"Is it such a crime to get drunk?" I asked.

"The men ain't allowed no booze," said the Corporal. "And while we're about it, that goes for you too."

I've seen many punishments, but for such a small crime this one seemed very cruel. They beat the man not with a stick, but with a flail made of strips of hide, which from the first stroke opened wounds on his back. Time after time the lash flayed the skin from his body, so that I had to look away. Eventually he fainted and his comrades lifted him from the ground still unconscious and carried him off. The crowd of watching soldiers slowly dispersed, shuffling away and muttering amongst themselves.

"That'll learn him," said Harrison with relish. "There won't be no more stealing from the stores now. You mark my words."

In the camp I met many black men from the other tribes I'd seen fighting under British command. They seemed to think that Zulus were haughty and domineering, and feared we meant them harm. They eyed me from a distance with fixed, cold expressions. Maybe I was wrong, but I felt safer with the white men than I did with them.

Black and white mostly didn't mix in the camp but perhaps the British made an exception for me because of my age. Usually the black fighters slept a little apart from the red soldiers, singing their own songs through the increasingly chilly nights. But Corporal Harrison liked having someone to run errands for him, and I was very happy to have his gruff protection for a while, and slept outside his tent.

He taught me how to aim a rifle, and I showed him how to throw a spear. It was a fair trade.

He fingered a throwing spear he'd collected from the battlefield.

"Beautiful!" he said, running his nail along the blade. "Look at the work that's gone into that!"

It looked like any other spear to me. "Yes. It takes many hours to make a spear," I said.

"Just to throw away?"

"We try very hard not to lose them," I said with a smile.

"I should think you do!" he replied.

"A rifle's much more complicated than a spear," I commented.

"Takes a fair old time to make one of these an'all," he said. "Only they're made in a factory. See!" And he showed me the maker's name – "Martini-Henry" – stamped on his firearm, and then told me what a factory was.

Every day there was something new that I asked to have explained to me ... newspapers, postage stamps, magic lanterns, cricket bats ... these men owned so many things!

Whenever there was a break from marching, cleaning, and digging latrines, the British soldiers played football or cricket. I easily understood football, and joined in, astonishing them with the way I could skip over and around the stony ground and then kick the ball with my bare feet. But in all my weeks with the British, I never did understand the rules of cricket. It seemed a long and pointless game.

A month or more passed and the men were becoming bored and restless. There were occasional fist fights about nothing in particular, when the officers weren't looking. If they were found out, there were repeats of the terrible flogging that I'd witnessed during my first few days in camp.

"Something's got to break," said Harrison one day in frustration. "You can't keep the men out 'ere on short rations for ever. They're fit to bloomin' explode. They want to do for old Cetyway-hay, and get back home to their wives."

"Cetshwayo," I corrected him. "The King's name is Cetshwayo."

He looked at me crossly. "All right, all right, keep your hair on."

"Will there be another attack?" I said, trying not to show how anxious I was.

"It ain't *if*, it's *when*." Harrison spat his plug of tobacco on the ground. He could make one plug last several hours. "I thought you knew that."

"What does the British Queen want with King Cetshwayo?" I asked.

"I don't know it's her so much, as the generals, and traders and such," Harrison answered. "They think if they can get him out of the way, the rest of you'll be no trouble."

His words stirred up the uneasiness that always lay sour and heavy in my stomach during those days. I wasn't British. But was I a loyal Zulu, if I tended the British cows? When the *umCijo* warrior had taunted me those few weeks ago I hadn't been a traitor, but what was I now?

Three days later, we struck our camp west of the *Mzinyathi*. Word had arrived that Colonel Wood was to march east into Zulu country, to rendezvous with Lord Chelmsford for an attack on Ulundi.

As the British army moved, I went with them, still not knowing what to do. Driving cattle into Zululand in the service of the British Queen, I felt worse and worse the further we travelled. Every day I felt more of a turncoat. We were more than a day's hard walk from kwaSihayo, but I was constantly afraid a face I knew would pop out of the grass and challenge me. What if it was Sipho? What would he say to me? I imagined our conversation, and the contempt with which he'd treat me. "*What are you doing, Jabulani?*" he'd say. "*Think of your family, and the shame you're bringing upon them!*"

But I felt loyalty to the British too. They could have killed me if they'd wished, but they'd shown me mercy, hospitality – even kindness. And the chilling words of the *umCijo* still lurked in the back of my mind. Was it possible he could find me, if ever I returned home?

Day after day we travelled to the east. Even where there was little or no water in the rivers, some days the column could make no headway at all because enough grass and foliage needed to be cut to provide a sure footing across the mud and sand of a river course.

119

More care was taken with the camps now. Each night a defensive ring of wagons surrounded us, a *laager* as the white men called it. At any one time, many of the men were ill, and had to survive the jolting journey as best they could on the boards of the carts, sweating and delirious. I helped dig graves for several soldiers for whom it all proved too much.

Finally the British army made a great camp on the Heights of Mtonjaneni. Several camps in fact, since more than one column of British troops had now joined forces. It was a place I remembered from my two journeys to Ulundi earlier in the year. Far in the distance to the north, in the valley beyond the fat python river of the White Mfolozi, I could just make out smoke rising from the great royal *kraal*. Even further to the east on a clear day I could imagine I glimpsed the glittering sea. Most days I certainly saw the blanket of warming cloud that rolled in from it. It was a magical, beautiful mountain. And nowhere have I felt unhappier.

The day after we arrived Harrison came to find me. I was with the herd, as usual.

"Hey you," he shouted. "The colonel wants you."

I'd seen very little of Colonel Wood in the past weeks. He'd stopped and talked with me once or twice, but he was a busy man, and I was one of many hundreds of people he might pass by in a day.

On a table outside his tent, overlooking the valley, lay a magnificent pair of ivory tusks. They'd once belonged to a prince among elephants. Beside Wood stood two men. They were scanning the valley with telescopes.

"*Ay-ih*," I said when I saw the tusks. I had seen only one pair like it in my life. In King Cetshwayo's palace.

"Extraordinary, aren't they?" said Wood turning to me. "You can guess who they're from, can't you, Jabulani?"

I lowered my head to show I knew.

"It's a peace offering," said Wood, "from your King Cetshwayo. And if you look down there –" he pointed into the valley – "you'll see more goodwill making its way towards us." He turned to one of the telescope men. "Let the boy have a peek, then!"

Reluctantly the man handed over his strange eyepiece. To my amazement I could see that in the valley two Zulus were driving a couple of hundred head of cattle towards the camp. In their rear strode a tall, powerful man in elaborate dress, attended by a handful of other unarmed men. I nearly dropped the precious telescope. It was Sigwelewele. I was sure of it. As I squinted through the glass, trying to get a better look, there was an interruption.

"Sir!" The other telescope man spoke urgently. "To the left, sir. Something's going on."

The telescope was snatched back, but even with the naked eye, I could see exactly what was happening. Another band of Zulus was rushing across the plain towards Sigwelewele and his cattle-gift. In a few minutes they were standing between the cattle and the hill, blocking his way. From the look of them, I guessed they might be *umCijo*, though I couldn't be certain at that distance.

"What do you make of it, sir?" said one of Wood's lieutenants.

"Well," Wood muttered, stroking his chin, "there's an argument going on, all right! I'd say it was likely someone on the Zulu side wants to make peace, and someone else wants to stop them."

Even while we stood watching the Zulus, a messenger rode in at full pelt and handed an envelope to the Colonel. He opened it, read the contents, smiled a little sadly, and crumpled the paper into a ball.

In front of everyone, he turned to me and said, "I'm sorry for troubling you, Jabulani. I'd thought your talent for speaking English was going to come in useful at last. But it seems Lord Chelmsford also has ideas other than peacemaking. Out there your King is not being allowed to *make* a peace offering by his own men, and in here I am not allowed to *accept* one."

He gestured towards the plain, where Sigwelewele was still disputing with the *umCijo*. "Instead I suspect we shall be talking only with weapons." He spread his hands. "I'm truly sorry."

In my heart I didn't know whether to be sorry or glad. The minute I had seen Sigwelewele through the telescope, my stomach had turned to water. The thought of having to act as a go-between for him and Colonel Wood was frightening. At least I was now spared having to hear what Sigwelewele might say to me.

It was just possible to see the great battle for Ulundi from Mtonjaneni. The British army marched and rode out, determined and organized, leaving the stores and the cattle safely behind them. Once they were down and across the river, they formed a great red square. Harrison and I watched the shape of it from above. He pointed out the cavalry and the lancers to me, hanging back a mile or so behind the mass of soldiers. They were being held in reserve, for the moment when the Zulu line began to crack, as the British were certain it would.

"I'd bet the Colonel didn't want it like this," Harrison said grimly, "but perhaps it's best to get it over and done."

"The Zulus will fight bravely," I said defiantly.

"They won't even get close," replied Harrison softly, matter of factly. "Lord Chelmsford wants revenge for Isandlwana. That's what this is all about."

Watching from that distant mountain, everything appeared to happen so very slowly. It was hard to know what we saw and what we imagined. The red square seemed to inch forward, its colour weakening as it moved further away from us. Beyond the British formation the surface of the ground became stubbled with black dots, as many as there are stars in the sky. These Zulu dots drew together and became a single mass, and the two armies closed on each other. Then little by little a dense cloud of smoke wrapped up the battlefield and hid the bloodshed from view.

Only when the cavalry rode back into camp, whooping their cries of triumph, their eyes still crazy with bloodlust, did we hear what had happened.

"A damn fine day's pig-sticking, Corporal Harrison, that's what!" hollered a young officer. "Excellent sport!"

He vaulted from his horse, and as Harrison held the reins of the exhausted animal, there was no stopping the officer from telling us what he'd seen. In lines hundreds of yards long, the Zulus had risen from the grass and advanced on the British guns, hoping to get close enough to put their stabbing spears to work. It was a hopeless cause. Rank after rank of our best warriors had been massacred in turn. It had been as if they had refused to believe that bullets could kill.

At some point, when the metal rain had become just too great to bear, and their courage had at last failed them, the *impi* turned and fled. Then the British cavalry had seized their opportunity. They'd charged in with lances and swords to chase the fleeing warriors over the open country. Hundreds had died the way animals die in a hunt, running till they could run no more, then bravely turning to face the final act rather than taking steel between the shoulderblades.

The next day a few British wounded were carried back into the camp. I found Harrison talking to one of them. His name was Adam and from his head flowed a cascade of blond hair which fascinated me. It was the colour of white sand from a river bank, bleached by months in the sun. He was propped up against a tree, gratefully smoking a clay pipe which Harrison had found for him. I was puzzled – I couldn't see what was wrong with him.

"Where are you shot?" I asked.

He laughed. There was contempt in the laugh, not just at a foolish question, but at me, simply because of who I was. He clearly had no time for black people, however good their English. "Shot? I ain't shot! Your people ain't ever shot any British soldier except by luck. Broke my ruddy ankle, didn't I, down some ruddy rabbit hole! When it was damn near all over and the darkies were running away too!"

His reply was spoken to Harrison, not me. The young soldier couldn't even bring himself to meet my gaze.

"What about the King?" pressed Harrison. "Did they find him then? Have they got him in chains?"

Sometimes the soldiers talked about how they would seize the King and what they'd do to him when they'd taken him, talk which I found very hard to hear. I'd heard dreadful things said about King Cetshwayo, how he would eat human flesh every night, how he had people killed for entertainment – things I knew were lies.

"They burned Ulundi good and proper," said Adam with satisfaction. "There ain't a grass hut standing. Nor anybody left to put it back together." He looked at me disdainfully. "The blacks are finished. Cowards the lot of them, when it came to it."

He hadn't answered Harrison's question.

"So the King's still free?" I probed.

Adam turned his shoulder away from me and continued to speak his answer only to Harrison. "Couldn't find him, or so I heard. Run down some little hole in the ground, no doubt. And you know what?"

Harrison shook his head.

"When they came to what they were pleased to call his 'palace', it weren't no more than a slightly bigger hut like all the rest. But they say the floor was littered with empty bottles of gin and champagne and the like! Now what do you make of that?"

"Go on!" said Harrison, genuinely surprised.

"They'll catch up with him, you see!" Now finally Adam looked round at me spitefully. "No black man's a white man's equal."

To do him justice, Harrison looked sheepish, although he said nothing to the injured man. I walked away and left them. In my time with the British army, most people had been gentle with me, though occasionally there had been unkind things said. Usually I told myself it was only to be expected. They were fighting a war against people who looked like me, after all. This time, Adam's words lay in my stomach and festered. The whole of the following day they churned around, until I made a decision to rid myself of them and my guilt, once and for all. I would just have to take my chances with the *umCijo*. Nothing was worth the way I had begun to feel.

Colonel Wood had ridden back into the camp that morning, and I went to find him. As usual, the flap of his tent was tied back, and he was sitting behind a portable writing table in the open air, in the shade of the canvas. His assistant fussed around him. I waited until he spotted me.

"Jabulani!" he said briskly. "What can I do for you?"

"I've decided I must go back to my people," I said. I wasn't asking permission, and I stood tall as I spoke.

He stopped writing and sat back in his chair. He looked me up and down. I thought he seemed tired. "Of course, Jabulani, you must do as you think fit." He paused. "If you're sure it's the right moment."

"Yes, Colonel Wood," I answered, giving him his full title. "I'm sure."

"You know you're welcome to stay on here?"

"It's good of you, Colonel Wood," I said. "But I've made up my mind to go."

"Very well, then!" He stood up. I felt suddenly shy and awkward.

"Thank you," I said, and turned to go.

"Wait," he called, and disappeared for a moment into his tent, returning with something held in his hand, which he pushed into mine.

"You're a brave and clever young man, Jabulani," he said. "May God go with you!"

When I opened my hand, I saw that he'd given me a bright, shiny medal, the kind he wore on the breast of his jacket. From the way he lingered slightly in parting with it, I think it must have been one of his own.

The soldier Adam was right. Very little was left of Ulundi. As I walked into the royal *kraal* it was late in the afternoon, and the sun was slipping from the sky, staining the clouds blood red. Although here and there a hut was still standing, most had been torched. Columns of smoke still rose from the last hot remains of grass and wattle, and between them wandered the shadows of a few dazed Zulus, shaking their heads, rubbing their eyes in disbelief. A woman sat by herself on the turf, rocking rhythmically from side to side, her arms locked together. From deep inside her came a melancholy moan, like the whining of wind through trees in a storm.

I picked my way through the sad debris to where King Cetshwayo's place of honour had been, right at the back of the royal *kraal*. I could see the outline of his quarters, piles of ash, odd discarded skins. If there'd ever been bottles of liquor in the huts, there was no sign of them now. I wandered around, not knowing what to do next. I poked with my foot at something lying half-covered by the ash, and as I did so heard my name called from behind me softly, questioningly. I jumped. I remembered the voice, dignified and grave.

"Jabulani, son of Sihayo, brother of Mehlokazulu? I'm right, aren't I?" the voice said.

"Themba!" I answered. It was the King's personal attendant. He seemed to have defied age. Now, away from the King's presence, he was apparently taller and more lively. We clasped hands. "I'm surprised you remember me!" I said, haltingly.

"Everyone remembers you," he said, apparently puzzled. "From the battle at Khambula."

I didn't understand, and dropped my head in shame. Only one thing was on my mind. "You don't by any chance have news of my family, do you?" I asked quietly. "My father? Is he dead? And the King? Is he dead too?"

"No, no," replied Themba. "There are many who have gone to the ancestors, but your father and Mehlokazulu are alive and with the King. I can take you to them, if you like."

My heart leaped for joy.

"I came back here for one last look," Themba said in a melancholy voice. "To see if there was any comfort I could take the King for the loss of Ulundi."

"There's nothing left," I said, shifting my foot through the dust and ashes on the floor of what had once been the royal hut. "Look at it!"

Themba jumped on to his haunches, and pulled from the ash the scraps I'd been kicking a few moments earlier.

"Not quite *nothing*," he exclaimed. "See!" He brandished aloft a tattered, matted mess of skin and cloth. Dirt fell from it, and he scraped off some more with his long delicate fingers, but I still couldn't make out what it might have been.

"This will bring the King joy," he said. "Real joy!"

"Will it?" I said doubtfully.

"It's an omen for better times. Listen! Many years ago, before all the trouble, the Queen of England sent this headdress to the King as a message of goodwill. She wears such a crown herself. The King has always held the gift in great esteem."

Themba rose to his feet.

"My journey hasn't been in vain," he said. "I told them it would be worth coming, and now it was. I can return with two surprises for them. This…" He waved the "crown" around. "And you…!"

As it happened, we came across Mehlokazulu first. He was waiting anxiously for Themba's return at the foot of a path which led up to a rough shelter clinging camouflaged to the side of a small valley. When he saw me he started to tremble.

"Jabulani?" he said. "It can't be!" Then, a second time, "Jabulani? Is it you? If you're a spirit, go away and leave me. I want no business with you. I mean no harm."

For a moment I thought he was joking, but then I saw he was quite serious. My brother thought I was a ghost.

"Mehlokazulu, it's me!" I said. "Really me! Flesh

and blood." But still he had to prod me to prove to himself I was real and no phantom, before he caught me up in his huge arms and greeted me properly.

"I thought you were dead," he whispered. "I saw you charge at Khambula, shouted at you to stop, lost you in the smoke. After the attack there were so many dead. It was terrible, Jabulani. They covered the ground like fallen leaves. And then we could never return to that place because of the covering fire from the red soldiers. You showed such bravery, little brother. I couldn't believe it was you. You were an inspiration to the Zulu warriors. If little Jabulani could do such a thing, they said, then surely they could face the white men's power with at least as much courage."

I didn't know what to say. Far from being a clumsy coward and a traitor, always in the wrong place at the wrong time, it seemed I'd become a hero. But in my heart I didn't believe it. Inside I felt small, timid and foolish.

During the next weeks the King's party, of which I was now an honoured member, became nomads in the bush of northern Zululand. It was a place of deep gullies, high cliffs, thickets of thorn: a very good place to hide. But we kept moving, fearing the King would be betrayed. Some of the Zulus living there had never liked Cetshwayo, and never accepted him as true King. And now even previously loyal subjects might find a reward for information very hard to resist. So every few days we pulled down our scanty shelters, covered our tracks and walked on to some new cave or gorge.

Every so often we would hear that red soldiers were looking for us.

"*They were asking about the King. Yes! Three men on horseback and a few more on foot, all well-armed!*" we'd be told when we passed some seemingly friendly little *kraal*. "*No, of course we'll say nothing if they come back. You can trust us!*" We weren't sure we could.

I learned more about hunting in those few weeks than in the rest of my life. The King and my father were out of practice. They hadn't thrown a spear for years and had never fired a rifle in their lives, so they weren't much use. The hunting was down to Mehlokazulu, myself and Themba. Despite his wrinkles it turned out Themba was surprisingly quick, and had immensely strong wrists and elbows. His spear travelled further than Mehlokazulu's.

Occasional visitors to our camps provided men for extra protection, and sometimes they brought us gifts of food, but mostly we caught our own. There was very little which didn't turn up in our pot – birds, wild boar, deer, rabbit, and every imaginable kind of root, leaf and mushroom.

But my clearest memory of that time is the silence. Every evening of my childhood I'd fallen asleep to the noise of singing, dancing and joking – a comforting pillow of sound. Now we talked the evenings through in hushed tones, not wanting to give away our hiding place. Sound travels a long way in the bush. Anyway we were sad, in mourning for what had been lost. And still I felt as if I was living a lie. They thought me a brave boy, and told me so very often. Inside I knew different, and shuddered at every word of praise.

One evening I remember my father being particularly gloomy.

"What will become of the Zulu people now?" said Sihayo. "We've never been slaves to anyone, but that's what the British want to make us. Those of us who are left, that is."

The King tried to rally him. "That's not like you, old friend," he chided. "They may have killed many Zulus, but Zulu spirit isn't going to roll over and die. Look at Jabulani! Out there in the darkness there are thousands more like him. We'll rise again, like a new moon, and perhaps just as quickly. You'll see."

But my father's shoulders stayed hunched. Even if the King believed his own words, my father showed he doubted them by his long face and his silence.

One day Mehlokazulu, Themba and I were in the bush, when we were surprised by a large *kudu*, which suddenly crashed through the grass and trees to our right. It was a fine animal, and meat was running low. Mehlokazulu threw his spear by instinct, though he was caught off balance, so near had the large deer passed to us. The weapon flew too low and late. It caught the beast high on a back leg so that it stumbled, but kept running. Usually a man is no match for a deer in flight, but we chased it at top speed, for once careless about where we went. Suddenly the grass cleared and we found ourselves trapped in the open, staring down the barrels of British army rifles aimed at us from two sides. The report of a gun from ahead of us indicated the last strides of the *kudu*.

There were half a dozen of them on foot and two on horseback. The man who seemed to be in command, swung himself down from his horse, and strode up to us. He spoke very good Zulu.

"You're Zulus?" he said.

"Of course," said Mehlokazulu.

"You know there's a reward for anyone with information on the whereabouts of King Cetshwayo?"

"*Ay-ih,*" sighed Mehlokazulu, playing the innocent, as if such an idea were very strange and wonderful. "Is that so?"

"You wouldn't happen to know where he is, would you by any chance?" probed the soldier, looking from Themba to Mehlokazulu and back again.

Perhaps some faint look in Mehlokazulu's eye gave the game away. Or perhaps the soldier just acted on a hunch. His voice suddenly became rougher. "You know something, don't you?" he asked harshly, his face almost up against Mehlokazulu's. I saw my brother flinch away from the man's sour breath.

"I don't know what you're talking about," he said. "I don't know anything."

With his eyes still glued to Mehlokazulu's, the officer said in English to his horseback companion, "This one knows something, I'm sure of it."

The other man leaped down from his saddle and came forward to inspect us more closely, peering at us one by one, searching for weakness.

The first man said to Mehlokazulu, "I'm going to ask you just one more time. Where is your King?"

This time Mehlokazulu said nothing at all.

"All right," said the officer. "Have it your way!"

He spoke to the soldiers. "Take him," he said, pointing to Themba, "and deal with him."

They took Themba's weapons from him and two of the soldiers led him away out of sight beyond the bushes. We waited. Nothing was said. A bird cawed loudly from a nearby tree. There was the rustling of wind, a distant roar that might have been a leopard, and then a single shot. Mehlokazulu blinked twice, three times. The officer gave time for what had happened to sink in. Mehlokazulu must have guessed what was coming next.

"Tell us what you know," said the red soldier. "Or I'll kill the boy."

I felt arms bind me from behind. Without thinking I whispered, "Don't say anything, Mehlokazulu. Don't give in. Remember what's important!"

The officer took a pistol from his belt, and I heard the click as it was cocked for action, felt the steel from its barrel pressed against my head just above the ear.

"I'll shoot him here while you watch, you black savage," shouted the red soldier. "One last chance! Talk!"

I felt the barrel move hotly against me, and was sure the moment of death had come. After what seemed an eternity, Mehlokazulu spoke in a mumble. "I'll take you to the King," he said. "Just let the boy go."

"No, Mehlokazulu," I said in despair. "No!"

With heads sadly bowed and shoulders drooping, we led the British soldiers into the bushes which hid the secret little valley where we'd camped that day. It was the worst moment of all, a feeling that we had completely failed, that life could never be the same again. My brother and I could scarcely bear to look at each other. The soldiers pulled the King triumphantly from his rough reed hut, and we waited for his scorn with heavy hearts.

But he had no harsh words for us. King Cetshwayo

accepted his arrest with quiet dignity, as if sooner or later it was inevitable.

"It's only him we want," said the officer with a smirk. "He's valuable goods, bound for Cape Town. The rest of you can do what you damn well like. But don't try anything if you value the King's life."

Thinking quickly, I stepped forward. "Let me stay with the King," I said. "He'll need someone to look after him."

The officer looked thunderstruck to be spoken to in his own tongue. He recovered himself and thought for a moment.

"Well, I suppose even an African king should be allowed at least one servant," the officer laughed to his companion, making fun of us.

I went forward to King Cetshwayo, and threw myself at his feet, as much for the benefit of the soldiers as anything else, to show them how a king should be treated.

"Wherever you go, I'll go," I said to him. "Let me be your *udibi*. Let me be your voice to the white man."

The King looked doubtfully at Mehlokazulu, who glanced at me and then bowed his head in agreement. "Well then, I accept your offer, Jabulani," the King said. There was a catch in his throat as he added, "I shall miss old Themba very much. But your company will be of great comfort."

He embraced Mehlokazulu. "Don't be troubled, son of Sihayo," he said gently. "In these last weeks, you have done everything you could, and then much, much more."

I felt a weight lift from my shoulders with his words. Though that day was one of great sadness and tragedy, at its end I was standing tall. For the first time since the battle of Isandlwana, I was finally at peace. I would make it up to my King and my people by serving them as best as I knew how.

And so months later, after journeyings and imprisonments, questions and parades, I find myself on the deck of a ship riding out to sea from the harbour at Cape Town. The ship is bound for England. They say we shall meet the British Queen there.

In the background lies a high mountain with a white hat of cloud sitting on its top. The sailors' name for it is Table Mountain. In its shadow lies a crowd of houses built from painted wood and stone. They still look very strange to me, a white man's *kraal* which leaves no space to breathe.

Before we left port the King had his photograph taken. He was very nervous of the camera at first, thinking it a weapon of some peculiar kind, until the ship's captain showed him photographs of other important people. Then he was most anxious that his picture should be taken too, portraying him as a Zulu warrior king should look: handsome, upright and proud in our traditional dress.

King Cetshwayo looks very different now. To

protect him from the cold sea winds he has put on the white man's clothes, and so have I. They feel rough and uncomfortable, and the waves scare me. At the moment I feel very ill, but I made my promise to go wherever the King goes, and I will not break it. He seems less affected by seasickness than I am, and says he enjoys the rolling and pitching of the ship in the tall waves.

We are in the power of the white men for the moment, but they cannot hold our spirits down. Their clothes are chains around them. They cannot live from the land as we do, or feel its rhythms. They do not dance, laugh and sing as we can. They do not speak with their ancestors. One day the King and I will come back from this journey. I will come back to the people I love, to the land I worship, and so will he. We will come back to the freedom that is ours by right.

Historical note

Whether it's a fight in the playground or a major war, understanding why two sides have fallen out and who's to blame can be very tricky. There's often no simple answer. Each side sees things differently. The excuses people offer for starting a fight and the real reasons behind their anger or fear are frequently not the same.

The *excuse* for the war between the British army and the Zulus in 1879 was the incident involving Kaqwelebana which you've read about early in this book. The British used it to lay an ultimatum to King Cetshwayo which they knew he couldn't accept.

The *reason* for the war was far more about money. Even today, Britain is a much richer and more powerful country than you'd expect for its size. Part of the reason for this is the energy which Britain has shown in trading all over the world. Sometimes, and particularly in the eighteenth and nineteenth centuries, it deployed its army to help things along. That's what happened in Zululand. The Zulus were simply in the way.

In the 1870s the British government took a very

aggressive attitude towards bringing together under one British rule all the various little colonies, republics and nationalities in the southernmost part of Africa. Their aim was to increase trade and profit for Britain. Needless to say, many of the different groups, including the Zulus, were unhappy with this. They might have respected and even liked the British, but they had their own traditions and pride. By acting as they did, the British government coiled up a chain of events which is still unravelling today.

The British who lived in Natal on the southern borders of Zululand knew that Zulu society was well-ordered, sophisticated and relatively open to new ideas. But some of them also saw this intelligence and confidence as a threat, particularly when it was coupled with travellers' tales of Zulu deeds in battle.

Zulu kings held complete power of life and death over their subjects. King Shaka revolutionized Zulu warfare 50 years before King Cetshwayo. He invented the *iklwa*, the stabbing spear, and encouraged the warriors to get in close to their enemies. The legendary crescent-shaped Zulu attack formation was also his. But at times Shaka had been a tyrant, executing opponents and even completely innocent people on a whim. He'd never been shy of intimidating other tribal groups with Zulu military might either. Although King Cetshwayo was a very different kind of man, peace-loving and calm, the warlike reputation of the Zulus lived on in European minds.

Nevertheless, in 1879 the British believed that the Zulus would never be able to stand up to their army, and when they first confronted them in the great battle at Isandlwana, it seems as if they didn't bother to prepare properly. The British troops went off to fight almost light-heartedly. Then disaster struck. The various commanders lost touch with each other in the crucial moments before the battle, and the Zulus were allowed to close on the British lines where their spears were put to devastating use. In later battles the British learned to keep the Zulus at a distance so that their superior rifles and cannon could cause havoc. Then it was the Zulus whose tactics were questionable and inflexible. Why did they keep running at the British guns in set-piece battles rather than using repeated "guerrilla" techniques to wear down their opponents?

Isandlwana was a very great shock to the British back home in London, and not even the heroic defence of the farmhouse at Rorke's Drift, where more soldiers won the Victoria Cross than at any single engagement before or since, could take away the pain.

The British government couldn't afford for things to go wrong again, and reinforcements were called in from around the world to make sure they didn't. The British army of the time was actually quite small compared with other European forces. It numbered just 186,000 in total, but these were spread thinly across many territories around the globe. The British were accustomed to using native soldiers to build up their forces, and they did so in Zululand too, but more than was sometimes the case, the burden now fell on the British "regulars".

Another round of battles at Hlobane and Khambula in March and April eventually went the British way, and finally Lord Chelmsford, the British commander-in-chief, found himself in a position to attack the Zulu capital at Ulundi on 4 July.

King Cetshwayo fled into the hills as Ulundi burned but was eventually captured and sent into exile at Cape Town, while the British divided up his kingdom between chiefs prepared to obey their new masters. In 1882, the King was allowed to visit England and even to meet Queen Victoria, before returning to Zululand the following year. He died just twelve months later, probably poisoned by a rival after a tribal dispute.

In the aftermath of the war, Zululand was largely

peaceful until 1906, when the British government decided to introduce a poll tax on all Zulus, at the same rate they'd applied to all Europeans living in Natal. There was just one difference. The Zulus were much, much poorer than the Europeans, and the effect of the tax on them was severe. It seemed very unfair, and so they rebelled. Exactly how many died is not certain: it may have been as many as 2,000, but we know that one of them was Jabulani's elder brother Mehlokazulu.

He and most of the characters in our book are historical – for instance: Nkubikazulu, Kaqwelebana, Sihayo, Sigwelewele, King Cetshwayo, and Colonel Wood.

But Jabulani and Sipho and the other young *udibi* are from my imagination, and so are Corporal Harrison and Themba.

Of the events you've read about in Jabulani's story, most are historically accurate. The action at Hlobane and Khambula was more complicated than I've made it sound. There were actually two battles fought, and the Zulus surprised and scattered the British in the first of them, at Hlobane.

King Cetshwayo *was* betrayed to the British, but slightly differently than I've described. A ruthless officer called Lord Gifford was in charge of the hunt for the King, during which he beat up and threatened many Zulus. He finally found a farm where it was thought the King had stayed the previous night. There were two boys there. He blindfolded them, and then pretended to shoot one, so that the other was persuaded to lead Gifford to the King.

Both sides behaved towards each other with extreme violence, but then killing can never be easy and clean. We've become strangely used to hearing about bombs exploding, without ever seeing the detailed effects. The spears and bayonets of the Zulu wars can sometimes seem particularly gruesome and terrifying by comparison, but really the results in pain and human misery are no different.

If you're interested in this era of Zulu and British history, there are lots of books about the subject, and even a society to join. But remember, although if you searched hard enough, you could find some accounts of what happened from a Zulu point of view, most of what has been written has been by British hands, seen through British eyes. Perhaps Jabulani's story will help to keep a balance.

By the way, as is the case with most English first names, most if not all Zulu names carry a meaning. Jabulani means "joy-bringer"!

Timeline

1787 Birth of Shaka.

1816 Shaka becomes King of the Zulus. He begins to reform and re-train the Zulu army.

1828 King Shaka dies, murdered by two of his brothers.

1844 Natal becomes a British Crown Colony. Many white settlers move in to farm the best of the land, but remain in peaceful relations with their Zulu neighbours to the north.

1873 King Shaka's nephew, Cetshwayo, finally succeeds to the Zulu throne at the age of 46. In an attempt to get the King to accept British authority, he is crowned on Queen Victoria's behalf by Theophilus Shepstone, the British Secretary of Native Affairs.

1876 Lord Carnarvon, the Secretary of State for the Colonies in Disraeli's government, appoints Sir Henry Bartle Frere to be the Governor of the Cape Colony. His mission is to bring all of southern Africa under a single British rule, so that the mineral riches of the continent – diamonds and gold – can be exploited.

March 1878 Lieutenant General Frederick A Thesiger,

Lord Chelmsford, becomes commander of the Imperial forces in South Africa. Frere tells him war with the Zulus is inevitable.

July 1878 Kaqwelebana and Sihayo's younger wife are killed by a raiding party led by Mehlokazulu. This is the excuse Frere has been waiting for. Now he can claim the Zulus are a danger to the Natal settlers.

December 1878 Frere issues his ultimatum to King Cetshwayo. It includes demands that the Zulu military system be scrapped, and then re-assembled only after negotiation with the British. The British know these are terms which the Zulus can never accept.

10 January 1879 The British army begins a full-scale invasion of Zululand – before the ultimatum has expired.

12 January British forces engage with members of Chief Sihayo's family in the gorge near their *kraal*. Nkubikazulu is killed.

22 January Battle of Isandlwana proves disastrous for the British. In a rearguard action at Rorke's Drift a group of British soldiers salvage some pride and show great heroism against repeated Zulu attacks.

12 March A thousand Zulu warriors overwhelm a British convoy at the Ntombe River. Elsewhere in Zululand, at Eshowe, there's a stalemate at the siege of Fort Pearson.

28 March Colonel Wood's men attack Hlobane, but are driven off.

29 March The Zulus attack Wood's base at Khambula but are defeated.

4 July Battle of Ulundi. King Cetshwayo flees.

29 August King Cetshwayo is captured by Lord Gifford, and taken by ship to Cape Town, where he's held under house arrest.

May 1880 Frere recalled to Britain.

July 1882 King Cetshwayo arrives in England, and meets Queen Victoria.

January 1883 King Cetshwayo returns to Zululand, and builds a new *kraal* at Ulundi.

8 February 1884 The King dies, probably poisoned.

1906 Poll tax rebellion by Zulus against British.

1910 Lord Carnarvon's dream comes true. The Union of South Africa is formed.

1934 Self-government for South Africa.

1961 South Africa becomes a republic, but the policy of apartheid ("separate development" for different racial groups) hardens.

1993 Majority rule constitution. Apartheid ended.

1994 Nelson Mandela becomes the first black President of South Africa.

Picture acknowledgements

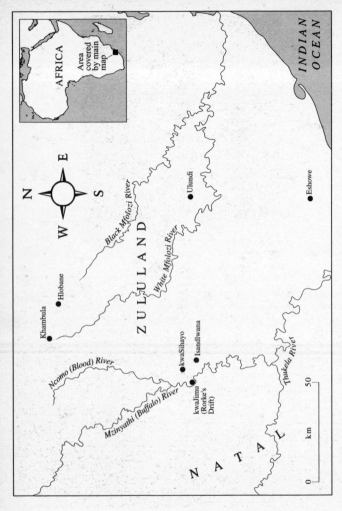

A map of Zululand and Natal showing many of the places mentioned in this book.

154

A painting showing a scene from the battle of Isandlwana.

This sketch shows Rorke's Drift the day after the British held out for many hours against a sustained Zulu attack.

A photograph of the British soldiers who defended Rorke's Drift in January 1879.

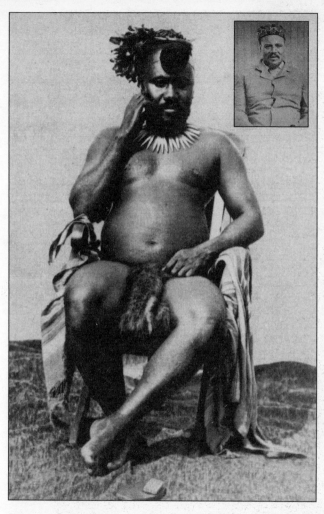

King Cetshwayo in his customary clothing. (Inset) Cetshwayo photographed in his Western suit during his visit to Britain.

Dabulamanzi pictured at Isandlwana with King Cetshwayo's brothers.

A group of Zulus photographed outside one of their huts.

Also in the series:

BATTLE OF BRITAIN
The Story of Harry Woods
England 1939-1940

THE TRENCHES
The Story of Billy Stevens
The Western Front 1914-1918

CIVIL WAR
The Story of Thomas Adamson
England 1643-1650

TRAFALGAR
The Story of James Grant
HMS Norseman 1799-1806

ARMADA
The Story of Thomas Hobbs
England 1587-1588

CRIMEA
The Story of Michael Pope
110th Regiment 1853-1857

INDIAN MUTINY
The Story of Hanuman Singh
India 1857-1858